W9-APS-760

Other books by
Colleen O'Shaughnessy McKenna:

CAMP MURPHY

Colleen O'Shaughnessy McKenna

AN
APPLE
PAPERBACK

SCHOLASTIC INC.
New York Toronto London Auckland Sydney

ISBN 0-590-45808-6

12 11 10 9 8 7 6 5 4 3 2 1   3 4 5 6 7 8/9

*This book is dedicated
with special thanks to
Mollie Scholtz and Matt Sheedy
for sharing their experiences
of their own backyard summer camps.*

Where would writers be without their readers?

Chapter One

"What?" Collette spun around quickly, and studied her best friend. "Sarah, you *can't* go to Ohio! What about our plans for Camp Summer Fun? We already have ten little kids signed up. Your name is on all the signs!"

"I know, Collette. Gosh, I sure don't *want* to go," cried Sarah. She bounced down next to Collette on the bed. "I would much rather stay in Pittsburgh and be a counselor for the camp. But my mom said the *whole* family has to go to Aunt Linda's wedding." Sarah pulled on her long red ponytail, looking miserable. "I don't even *know* this guy my aunt is marrying. She met him on a cruise ship. My mom says Aunt Linda would be

1

hurt if we didn't all go to wish her good luck."

"Well, *I* don't wish her good luck," grumbled Marsha. "We've been planning this camp all summer long, Sarah. You said you were going to teach the campers how to paint T-shirts using berries." Marsha flopped down on the bed next to Collette and Sarah. "Boy, it isn't *fair* that you have to leave town just when our camp is about to start. In fact, it *stinks*."

Collette glanced at Marsha. Marsha always got upset easily, but this time Collette couldn't blame her. The three of them had been planning a neighborhood summer camp for weeks. Summer vacation was almost half over and they were getting tired of swimming and bike riding. Having a backyard camp for little kids would be exciting. Plus, they would be able to earn some money.

The camp was scheduled to start on Monday morning and end on Friday afternoon with lots of awards and prizes for the campers. Being allowed to have the camp was a celebration of the three girls getting such good grades in the sixth grade.

"A neighborhood camp is a terrific idea," Collette's mother had said. "Just make sure it's before August fifth. I don't want to have the baby while a scavenger hunt is going on in my backyard."

Collette sighed. If Sarah went to Ohio, she wouldn't be able to work at the camp, teaching campers to make Rice Krispie treats or macaroni necklaces. Collette knew her little brother Stevie would really be upset. He was only five years old and loved the way Sarah could do backward flips and five cartwheels in a row.

Collette glanced at the bright yellow poster advertising their camp that was taped to her closet door.

Camp Summer Fun!!!!

Don't let your summer kid
drive you nuts!
Send that bored little child to us!
Activities, Crafts, Games and more...
For kids eight years old,
down to four!!!

Counselors: Sarah Messland,
Marsha Cessano and
Collette Murphy!!!!
Professional Baby-sitters!!

3

Monday, July 10th through Friday,
July 15th
Hours: 9:00-12:00
1408 Browning Rd.
(Collette Murphy's Backyard)
Very cheap, very fun, and very
organized
A real mother on duty to help
counselors
at all times
call 555-5673

"Oh phooey, Sarah. It just won't be the same without you," Collette said softly. The thought of crossing out Sarah's name on all the posters was depressing. Sarah was her best friend. Marsha was nice, too, but Marsha was more *neighbor* than friend. Marsha was fun to be around . . . unless she was in a bad mood. But Collette didn't share the same closeness with Marsha that she felt for Sarah. Sarah and Collette thought alike about so many things that they hardly ever disagreed. Not fighting always made a friendship a lot easier.

"Sarah, I wish we could just start camp when you get back, but lots of parents have already made plans. Two moms hired baby-sitters to pick up kids from camp. If we change the date, they might cancel."

Sarah nodded. "I know. Besides, I saw your mom downstairs. Boy, she sure looks pregnant. I bet the baby comes tonight."

Collette laughed. "She's not due for at least three more weeks. I can hardly wait." Collette felt her cheeks flush, remembering when the idea of her mother being pregnant with the fifth child sounded so awful. Luckily, *that* feeling lasted only a short time. Now, the whole family was excited.

"My mom wouldn't want to delay it," explained Collette. "She gets a little more tired every day."

"Tell her to send your crazy brothers and little sister to your grandmother's for a month," giggled Marsha. "I saw Jeff tying Stevie to a fire hydrant on my way in."

"They better stay out of sight when our camp starts," warned Collette. Her brothers spent most of their time chasing each other and making a lot of noise.

"I like your brothers. They're neat. In fact, I promised Stevie I would teach him to do a flip this week," said Sarah. "I'm going to miss all the fun." Sarah hugged Collette's lumpy stuffed cat. "I want to stay in Pittsburgh so badly."

Marsha blew her bangs straight up in the air. "Holy moley . . . an entire summer camp company is about to sink, Sarah. Just because your Aunt Linda wants to get married. . . *again!*"

Sarah sat up, her eyes beginning to shine with tears. "Marsha, how do you think *I* feel? I reminded my mother camp starts on Monday. I filled one whole notebook with ideas: a scavenger hunt, beaded necklaces, and. . . ." Sarah drew in a deep breath. "Oh well, at least my mom brought the craft things over, Collette."

"Thanks, Sarah. I'll write you every night and tell you all about the camp," promised Collette.

Sarah smiled. "Every night, Collette."

Marsha leaped off Collette's bed and yanked Sarah onto her feet. "Hey, we aren't giving up without a fight, are we? Forget the letter writing. I have a better idea, Sarah. Let your family go to Ohio and you stay here with *us* in Pittsburgh."

Collette laughed. Nobody could think faster than Marsha in a crisis. "Marsha's right. You can stay with me. You can have the top bunk and Laura can sleep in her pink sleeping bag by the window. My mom wouldn't care. She loves you."

Sarah smiled. "Thanks, Collette. I suggested that to my parents last night. I mean, I knew your mom wouldn't care since four kids live here already. My mom said your mom has enough to do right now."

"So, stay with *me* then, Sarah," Marsha said. "My mom isn't a bit pregnant. And since we're both only children, you would feel right at home. My bedroom VCR has remote control."

Sarah stood up and shook her head. "Sounds fun, Marsha. I wish I could. Last night my mom decided to make this some sort of family reunion. She's been on the phone all day with cousins and uncles that she hasn't seen in ten years. My grandmother hired some fancy photographer to take a group picture." Sarah shook back her ponytail. "Just promise me we can do the camp again next year, guys. And write me lots of letters." Sarah reached into her back pocket and handed Collette a folded square of white paper. "We'll be staying at my grandma's."

Collette tacked the address up on her bulletin board. "Remember that I'll write to you every night."

"Me, too," promised Marsha. "And we'll do such a great job with the camp that we'll have twice as many kids next year."

Sarah grinned. "You guys are great."

"I'll tell Stevie you'll teach him lots of tricks when you come back," promised Collette. "And I'll remind the parents that you'll definitely be counselor at camp next year."

"Unless your Aunt Linda decides to have a baby," grumbled Marsha. "Will you all have to go back to help her celebrate *that*?"

Collette and Sarah started to laugh.

Sarah opened the bedroom door. "Well, I better go now. My mom is waiting. Don't forget to write me."

Collette grinned. "All the news that's fit to print."

Collette and Marsha followed Sarah down the stairs in a quiet line. They watched as Sarah walked out the side door and got into her mother's green station wagon.

"Poor Sarah," Collette whispered as Sarah's car backed down the driveway.

"Poor Sarah phooey!" snapped Marsha. "Poor *us* is more like it."

Collette's eyes flew open. Had Marsha already forgotten how upset Sarah had been? "Marsha . . ."

Marsha leaned back against the wall and rolled her eyes. "Since Sarah backed out at the last minute, we are stuck with a huge problem, Collette."

Collette groaned. Sometimes it seemed Marsha enjoyed inventing *huge* problems, just so she could solve them ten minutes later and walk around like a hero. "So what's the big problem?"

Marsha took a step closer and grabbed Collette's arm. "The problem is that on all our signs, we promised *three* counselors. Right now we only have two counselors, which makes us liars. Mothers won't leave their kids with liars."

Collette's heart started to beat faster. Marsha sounded like she knew what she was talking about. What if she were right and Camp Summer Fun closed before it had a chance to open?

Chapter Two

"Our camp has got to open on Monday, Marsha," Collette announced. "Let's go up to my room where we can think."

As Collette raced up the stairs and hurried down the hall, she could hear her younger brothers laughing and thumping behind their closed bedroom door. Once Stevie and Jeff started wrestling, they usually stayed at it until they wore each other out. And Collette's little sister, Laura, was at a birthday party until four o'clock. That gave Collette and Marsha hours for planning. Plenty long enough to come up with a replacement counselor.

"I'm just being realistic, Collette. Our camp will *never* open." Marsha slumped down in Collette's yellow bean bag chair. "And I already bought a sterling silver whistle."

"You're the one who's being unrealistic, Marsha," said Collette as she closed the door. "Finding a new counselor can't be that hard. All we have to do is to get out our class picture and pick someone who lives nearby."

Collette reached for a picture on her bookcase. "Hey, how about Lorraine, or Peggy?"

"No way." Marsha sat up and shook her head. "They're nice in school, but both of those girls would drive me nuts if I had to spend a whole week with them."

"Why? They're okay. I like them."

Marsha leaned over and grabbed a tablet and a pencil from Collette's desk. "I *like* them. But that's not enough, Collette. We need a real kid expert." Marsha patted herself on her back. "Like the two of us, of course." Marsha pointed her pencil at Collette. "The key to having a great camp staff is all in the *chemistry*, Collette. That's why Sarah was so perfect. She knew how to handle kids, and she always agreed with me . . . I mean, us. We need someone who won't try to take over the whole camp. We need someone who will listen to

11

me, I mean us." Marsha grinned. "Trust me, Collette. It's all in the chemistry."

"Well, I hope we can find someone who's chemically correct." Collette smiled. "I want this to be the best summer camp yet!" Collette looked again at the class picture. Thirty-two sixth-graders smiled back at her. Marsha was sitting in the very center of the group. Every year she raced for the center seat. Behind her stood Collette and Sarah. Collette felt sad all over again, missing Sarah. Sometimes Marsha got a little bossy. She always wanted to be in charge of everything. Last week, Collette and Sarah had convinced Marsha that all of them should be in charge, in equal amounts. But now that Sarah was gone, maybe that rule would disappear, too.

"Let me see that picture, Collette." Marsha grabbed it. "Hey, how about Jessica? She's good in art and she likes to sing. Or, what about Kim and Kara? We could probably get two twins for the price of one."

Collette shook her head. "Jessica's staying with her uncle for the whole month of July, and the twins always go to camp for eight weeks."

"Phooey." Marsha ran her finger along the faces

in the picture. "Okay, how about Vanessa? She's so funny."

"She's going to Disney World on Sunday."

Marsha groaned. "Holy cow, doesn't *anyone* stay home anymore?" Marsha tapped her finger against the picture and started to laugh. "Now, I would love to hear that goofy Roger Friday was booked on a one-way flight to the moon. What a jerk!"

Collette laughed. "He's not a jerk, Marsha. I like him." Collette knew Marsha wouldn't agree with her. Marsha and Roger had been arguing with each other since the first day of kindergarten.

"We sure don't need Roger Friday!" snapped Marsha. "His chemistry is straight out of Dr. Frankenstein's lab."

"Roger would be a great counselor. He still thinks like a little kid."

"Yeah, too bad he still *acts* like one. Roger belongs in a metal cage with a rubber bone and a flea collar." Marsha pointed to another student. "Now, if you want to talk about someone with perfect chemistry, feast your eyeballs on Mr. John McKechnie. Let's ask him to volunteer for the job of counselor. If I could stare at his face all day I

13

would be in heaven. Boy . . . look at those eye-lashes! Look at that smile!"

Collette peered over Marsha's shoulder. Marsha was right. John McKechnie was the cutest kid in the whole school. Maybe the world. But Collette didn't know if he even *liked* kids. A good camp counselor had to know a lot about kids, practically *everything*.

Marsha grinned at the picture. "I think John has all of the qualifications. He's cuter than any-one in the world, and he turned twelve right before Christmas. Let's ask him."

"Marsha! There's no way John McKechnie would agree to be part of our little backyard neigh-borhood summer camp."

Marsha hopped off the bed. "Well, hey . . . *I'm* cool and *I* agreed to be a counselor."

"Well, that's different. Besides, Marsha, I don't even know if John *likes* kids," pointed out Collette. "The reason we decided to have our camp was because we knew so much about kids, right? I mean, I hate to brag, but we really do know kids pretty well."

Marsha leaned back against the bed and fanned her face. "But of course, dar-ling. We are wonderful persons." Marsha sat up and started to laugh. "But we also know a lot about chemistry, which is why we have to snag John McKechnie!"

"But does he understand kids as well as we do?" asked Collette. "Does he know what makes them tick?"

"Sure he does. John *loves* kids," Marsha said quickly. "He's on bus patrol, isn't he?"

Collette nodded, hoping that Marsha was right. Camp Summer Fun meant so much to her. She had wanted to start her own neighborhood camp ever since she was eight and her old baby-sitter, Molly Scholtz, started a camp in her backyard. It ran every summer until Molly went to college. Collette smiled. Maybe *her* summer camps would get so famous that Collette would end up on TV, telling everyone how she got her first real start with a tiny little neighborhood camp that led her straight to the White House in charge of the whole United States' summer camps and . . .

"Yoo-hoo, Earth to Collette, come in please!" Marsha knocked on Collette's head.

"Sorry!" Collette blinked and started to laugh. "I guess I was just daydreaming about how great our camp is going to be."

"*If* we can convince John to help us," reminded Marsha. "We need his chemistry. Let's get him over here."

"But we aren't even set up yet," said Collette. She pulled back her curtains and studied the backyard. It didn't look a bit like a camp right now.

"We'll be set up by tomorrow," promised Marsha. "My dad is bringing over two huge ice chests when he gets home tonight. And my mom went to a cool Italian store and got all this neat looking macaroni to make necklaces. And my Aunt Bernice is loaning us some of her white plastic lawn chairs in case some parents want to sit and watch us being terrific with their kids."

Collette grinned. Even though Marsha was an only child, she was great with kids, too. Once they came up with another counselor, Camp Summer Fun was going to be a snap!

"We can use our old blue tent for storytelling," said Collette. "And once we blow up the balloons and set up the craft tables, the camp will look really great."

Marsha wiggled her eyebrows up and down. "Yeah, that's why we've got to go call John

McKechnie." Marsha pulled Collette toward the door. "Come on, Collette. What's John's phone number?"

"*I* don't know," said Collette. "I think it's unlisted."

Marsha shook her head. "No, sometimes I open the phone book and just stare at it. Come on, let's hurry up before I lose my nerve."

Collette laughed. "How do you know he has the right chemistry?"

"John's chemistry should be bottled and sold in Saks." Marsha marched down the hall. "This camp is going to be so great. Wait till I write Sarah and tell her who's going to replace her. I'm going to bronze John's whistle and set it on my dresser."

"Wait a minute, Marsha. Shouldn't we . . . well, rehearse what we're going to say to him?"

Marsha was already in Collette's parents' bedroom, dialing. "I can handle it, Collette. Just watch me." Marsha grinned at Collette and fanned her flushed face. "It's ringing . . . oh hello." Marsha wrapped the phone cord around her wrist and rolled her eyes. "Hello, I mean, hi . . . is John in, there . . . I mean . . . like . . . home?" Marsha bit her lip and tugged at her bangs. "What? Who am I? Well . . ." Marsha looked up at Collette. "She wants to know who I am."

Collette groaned. "Well, tell her!" hissed Collette.

"Oh, who am I? Well, yes, I'm Marsha . . . Marsha Cessano. I'm your neighbor. I live in that real big house on the corner, well, it's not that . . . but, what I mean is, I go to school with your cute, I mean, son, John. He knows me. Is he there?" Marsha tugged on her bangs and shook her head into the phone. Finally, she looked up and smiled at Collette. "She's going to see if he's back from tennis."

Collette sat on the edge of her parents' bed. "Remember to be extra polite, Marsha. And stop babbling."

Marsha swatted Collette's ponytail. "I never babble."

"Tell him it starts at nine o'clock so be here . . ."

Marsha covered Collette's mouth as she started to talk. "Oh, hi . . . hi John." Marsha pushed her bangs straight up. "I guess you're back from tennis . . I mean, unless you're talking from your bike phone . . . ha, heh, ha . . . what? Who is this . . . well, it's me. Marsha."

Collette groaned. John probably thought he was getting a crank call. Boys got a lot of them in the sixth grade.

"Yes, Marsha Cessano. Listen, John, let me get to the point here." Marsha drew in a deep breath. Collette had never seen Marsha's cheeks so fiery red. "I thought up a little summer camp. You know, little campers come and I teach them to make crafts and sing songs . . . yeah, well thanks. It *is* a good idea, isn't it?"

"Marsha!" hissed Collette.

"And Collette helped with some of the thinking. In fact, I already asked her to be a counselor," added Marsha quickly. "And Sarah Messland *was* going to help, but her mom is forcing her to go to Ohio for the week, and now we need another counselor. Would you like to be one?" Marsha was quiet, nodding into the phone. Collette studied Marsha's face, wondering what John was saying. "Well, no big boys. I mean, of course there will be *little* camper boys there, but you will be the only *big* camper boy." Marsha rolled her eyes and shook her head at Collette. "I mean, you aren't a little boy, but you are a *big* boy . . . I mean a big counselor . . . I mean . . . ."

19

Collette yanked the phone away from Marsha. If Marsha talked to John any longer, he might hang up! "Hi, John, this is Collette."

"Hi."

"John . . . tomorrow, I mean, on Monday, Marsha and I will be starting Camp Summer Fun week. Parents are going to pay us to entertain their kids for the morning. Marsha and I wondered if you would help us." John wasn't saying anything on the other end of the line. Maybe he thought the whole camp sounded corny. Collette drew in a deep breath. "The little kids would like you. You're nice and real good in sports."

"Thanks."

"You're welcome." Collette wrapped the phone cord around her wrist. Since John was only giving one word answers, it was hard to tell if he was excited about the camp or not. "You'd make money and be finished by noon every day."

"Oh, really? How much?"

Collette grinned. Maybe John was getting interested. He was up to two-word sentences now.

"Maybe forty or fifty dollars," Collette said quickly. "We're charging ten dollars a kid for five mornings of camp. Our parents said we can't take more than fifteen kids, but we already have ten signed up. Marsha's mom and my mom are going to take turns staying close by in case we need an adult."

Marsha was grinning and nodding her head quickly. Collette knew that Marsha would give John her own share of the camp money if that's what it took to get him as a counselor. Marsha licked her fingers and started raking her bangs down, as if John were on his way over.

"So, would you like to be a counselor?" Collette hoped he would say yes. The campers could learn a lot about basketball from John, and Marsha would be in a guaranteed good mood all week.

"I don't know," John replied. "Little kids can be tough sometimes. My aunt's little kid throws food at everyone. And the girl who lives next door bit my dog's tail last Saturday."

Collette frowned. John sounded like he was getting ready to say no. "Well, our campers wouldn't do that. And it won't be hard work. Marsha and I will tell you what to do." Collette bit her lip. "I mean, if you want us to tell you. Of course we won't boss you around or anything, but if you get stuck, we'd help."

Collette drew in a deep breath. She was beginning to sound just like Marsha.

John laughed. Collette's heart started to beat faster. She couldn't remember if she had been trying to be funny or not.

"Well, I think the camp sounds cool," said John. "And I've been saving up money for a new tennis racket. Oh gosh, wait a minute. I don't think I can. Roger and I reserved a court on Bunker Hill to play tennis every morning. The city has a championship in August and we have to get ready."

Collette kept nodding into the phone.

"Did he hang up on you?" whispered Marsha. She looked terrified.

"Can't you get a new court time?" asked Collette. "You'd earn money for the new tennis racket, wouldn't you?"

"Yeah, and forty or fifty bucks would really help." John was quiet for another minute. "Collette, I'll try to switch our court time. But, can Roger be a counselor, too? He really likes kids, and we could walk down to Bunker Hill from your house."

"Roger Friday?" repeated Collette.

"WHAT?" Marsha sputtered into the phone. "Roger Friday?"

Collette yanked the phone back to her ear. "Sorry, John." Collette glared at Marsha. Just when they almost had him signed up, Marsha was going to scare him away.

"We'd have to split the money four ways," explained Collette. That wouldn't bother her so much. She just wanted to have the camp. Knowing a lot about kids was her only talent. She had to develop it, no matter what. Maybe including Roger was their only chance. "I'll call Roger right now and ask him."

"Over my dead body!" wailed Marsha. John laughed on the other end of the phone, while Marsha flopped down, face first, on the double bed.

"So, if Roger will do it, can we count on you, John?"

"Sure," agreed John. "And I just thought of something. Want me to bring four red shirts for us to wear? My dad has a whole box left over from his bowling tournament. They're in the garage."

"Great!" Collette knew how upset Marsha would be about having Roger on the staff, but she would be thrilled to wear a shirt that John gave her. Besides, camp *was* starting on Monday and they needed counselors, even if one of them had to be Roger Friday.

"Okay," said John. "You call Roger and I'll try to switch the court time." John's voice sounded cheerful, like he was really starting to like the idea. "In fact, do you want Rog and me to walk over to your house? To take a look at the camp and stuff?"

Collette paused. So far there wasn't anything to see. But she didn't want to tell John that. He might back out if he knew Camp Summer Fun still looked like the Murphy's backyard.

"Sure," she said slowly. "When?"

John was quiet for a second. "An hour?"

"An hour?" Collette's voice rose to a squeak.

Marsha lifted her face from the bed. "Is John coming here? In an hour?" She sat up and brushed back her hair.

"I'll bring the bowling shirts," said John. "They say 'Lucky Strikers' on the front."

"Thanks. Bye!" Collette hung up the phone and sat down on the bed next to Marsha. Things were starting to happen quickly now. Camp Summer Fun was like a giant train chug-chugging out of

24

the station. Camp was back on track, but Collette couldn't help but feel a little nervous. The "Lucky Strikers" shirts might help. Because with Marsha and Roger on the same staff, Camp Summer Fun was going to need all the *luck* it could get!

Chapter Three

"I am *so* happy Roger agreed to be a counselor," said Collette.

"And I am so *tired*," groaned Marsha. "Can't we stop now? I wanted to wash my hair before John gets here."

"Forget your hair, Marsha," said Collette. "They're going to be here any minute and I want things to look nice."

Marsha giggled. "Yeah, well, I want to look nice, too, Murphy."

Collette leaned against the tree and studied the yard. They had been working for forty-five minutes and had managed to borrow and drag Mrs. Cillo's umbrella table and chairs down the street and wash off Stevie's bright yellow plastic sandbox and turtle green wading pool. Next they had set the wading pool in the sun and lined up the sand toys in a neat row. Marsha was rinsing off the Murphys' picnic table now, and Collette still had to find a box big enough for the basketballs and Nerf footballs.

Collette stared up at the sky. The afternoon had gone so quickly. A bead of sweat trickled down her back; she was very tired. There was still so much to do. She reached down and gathered up the green and orange plastic Japanese lanterns left over from a summer barbecue, then stood on a picnic bench to hang the lights from the trellis to the rain gutter on the side of the house. She looked around the yard and smiled. The lanterns helped a lot. "Well, what do you think, Marsha? Does it look like a summer camp yet?"

Marsha looked up and studied the yard. Then she shook her head. "Not really. It looks like you're having a bunch of your relatives over for a cookout!"

Collette slid down on the picnic bench and studied the backyard. Marsha was right. "Okay, let's try to put up the big blue tent. We can read the campers a story in there every day, right before snack. The kids will love it. And, Marsha, why don't you run up to my room and get the story-telling sign? We can nail that to the tree beside the tent."

"How are we going to put up that huge tent?" asked Marsha. She slapped at a mosquito. "I can't even roll up my sleeping bag."

"We'll wait for the boys, then. Roger will know how to set it up."

"Roger Friday never has his *shoes* tied, Collette. He won't be a help at all. I still can't believe he is going to be a counselor." Marsha grabbed a bag of balloons and blew up an orange one. She knotted it and let it float in the middle of the birdbath. "I bet he agreed to do it just to make my life miserable. The only reason I am letting him set foot in *my* camp is because I want John here. It's like my mom always says, sometimes you've got to take the thorns to get the rose."

"First of all, Marsha, it is *our* camp. And secondly, Roger is not a thorn. Give the kid a break. The little kids will like him. He's funny."

Marsha closed her eyes. "*Oh, pleeeassse.* You wouldn't think that kid was so funny if he tormented you like he does me. I just know he will do something dumb and ruin our whole camp. Boy, if Sarah were here, she'd insist that Roger stay far, *far* away."

Collette stood up and pulled Marsha to her feet. "If Sarah were here we wouldn't need John or Roger, Marsha. Now come on and let's get busy. Roger and John will be here soon and we still have a lot to do. I'll get the tent and you get the sign and then start setting up the horseshoes. Tape the big green sign on the table. We can take it down after the boys leave, but at least it will give them an idea of how great things will look Monday. Oh, and Marsha, maybe you should sweep the driveway before . . ."

"Okay. Okay . . . holy cow, Collette. Slow down, I can't do everything." Marsha raised an eyebrow and frowned at Collette. "I mean, you are not the only one in charge here. I can tell you what to do, too." Marsha crossed her arms. "Like maybe you can go get the yellow buckets for the water balloon toss."

"Sure." Collette answered as cheerfully as she could. She wanted Marsha to know she viewed the camp as a *team* project. Everyone was in charge and no one was in charge. That seemed to be the fairest way. "Marsha, this is going to be so cool. I think we really do have some great ideas to keep the campers busy. We should make a list of things we will do every morning, just like in school. Maybe we could sing a good morning song, and then do the Pledge of Allegiance and — "

"There you go again, Collette. Stop thinking of everything all by yourself." Marsha picked up a tablet and started to write. "Okay, after the pledge, we will take roll, to make sure we didn't lose a kid already, then . . ." Marsha squinted her eyes and stared off into space. "Then, maybe ask each kid what he had for breakfast." Marsha broke into a huge smile. "We'll make this educational, too. If the kid says he ate cereal with a banana, we'll tell him he ate a good breakfast. If he only ate two cookies and a can of grape soda, we can remind him he had a crummy breakfast."

Collette frowned. "But we can't say it that way, Marsha. We don't want to hurt their feelings."

Marsha sighed and slapped the tablet down on the picnic table. "I know *that*. Just because I'm an only child doesn't mean I don't know *anything* about children, Collette."

"Marsha, I didn't say — "

"You think you are some sort of kid expert just 'cause your mom has so many. Now that your mom is about to have *another* one, you'll probably get even worse." Marsha shook her head. "I have lots of nieces and nephews, which is technically pretty close to brothers and sisters."

"I never said I was an expert." Collette turned around and moved the picnic benches closer to the table. She wasn't going to say another word. Boy, too bad Sarah wasn't here. She would make Collette laugh. Marsha could get her so mad. Besides, Marsha didn't really know *that much* about little kids. She spent most of her time with adults who treated her as if she were perfect.

Collette shook her head. Anyone who knew anything about kids knew nieces and nephews weren't *one bit* like brothers and sisters. Relatives went home.

Marsha never had to wait in line to take a shower, or almost miss the bus because she was helping a little sister find a missing tennis shoe, or let her own breakfast get cold while she helped cut up a little brother's French toast. Collette lifted her blonde ponytail, hoping for a breeze. The heat was turning her into a grouch. The truth was, she loved being the oldest child, the big sister. And when the new baby came, it would be even crazier and more fun.

Collette raced into the cool garage for the buckets. This week was going to be a lot of fun. She could hardly wait until Monday morning when neighborhood mothers would walk their children up the driveway and hand them over. "Take care of my precious child, Collette," they would beg. "I trust you completely!" Sure, some of the little kids might cry like they did on the first day of kindergarten. But Collette would show them all the wonderful activities, and by the time the parents came to pick them up, the little campers would probably refuse to leave. "I love Camp Summer Fun!" they would cry over and over again, their tiny little arms locked tightly around Collette's knees.

"I don't want to go home."

Collette laughed out loud. Camp was going to

be the best idea she had ever had. Each year she could add more and more kids and more and more counselors. Maybe her camp would become so popular buses would drive around with huge billboards advertising it.

Collette decided to borrow her dad's old basketball clipboard and start writing down the special talents of each counselor. John could play basketball in the driveway with the older kids, while Roger and Collette painted faces, and Marsha taught the campers how to make s'mores.

"Collette!"

Collette looked up. Her mother waved from the back porch. "Girls, you are doing such a nice job."

"How does my craft table look, Mrs. Murphy?" asked Marsha. "On Monday I'll tape red balloons on the sign."

"Looks great. I have a green plastic tablecloth in the garage if you want to use it. It's waterproof in case it rains."

"Mom, it isn't *allowed* to rain all week," reminded Collette. She grinned as her mother walked over to help them move the craft table under the shade tree.

"Be careful, Mom. Let me do most of the lifting," warned Collette. She didn't want to take any chances of hurting the baby.

Mrs. Murphy stopped and put both hands on her stomach.

"Are you okay, Mom?"

"Fine, fine. This baby must be doing somersaults." Mrs. Murphy smiled at Collette and Marsha. "Girls, I just got off the phone with Mrs. Lister. Do you have room for two more children?"

"If they're paying real money, we can *make* room," Marsha said.

Collette walked over to the picnic table and picked up her tablet. She flipped through the pages till she came to one marked REGISTRATION. "We can't take more than fifteen kids, since we only have one adult helping." Collette looked up, puzzled. "Mom, Mrs. Lister already signed up her two little boys. How many children does she have?"

Mrs. Murphy brushed off her hands. "Five-year-old and seven-year-old boys. But she has taken in two foster children."

"Foster kids?" Marsha looked curious.

"Yes," said Mrs. Murphy. "The children's father died a few years ago, and now their mother is unable to care for them. A social service agency asked Mrs. Lister to be their foster parent for the summer."

"Is she adopting the two kids?" asked Collette.

"No, she's not adopting them," explained Mrs. Murphy. "The foster children need a place to stay until their mother can take care of them."

"But, why do they have to stay with strangers? Don't they have relatives?" asked Collette. She shivered, thinking of how scared she would be to have to live with someone she had never met before. Looking up at her mother, she remembered how sad she had been when her mother had to stay in bed for two weeks because of her pregnancy. But even then her mother had just been upstairs. Collette had been able to talk to her and kiss her good night.

Mrs. Murphy looked at both girls. "I don't know the whole story, Collette. Mrs. Lister is so nice. I'm sure the children will enjoy their stay. Should I call her back and tell her to send the children on Monday morning?"

"Sure, I guess," said Marsha. "But, I've never even *seen* a foster kid before. Do you think they're sad all of the time?"

"Probably," said Collette. "Wouldn't you be? Marsha, listen, we have to be *extra* nice to those kids. But don't keep watching them, and don't yell if they try to eat all the snacks." Collette's cheeks flushed. The poor little kids didn't need Marsha staring at them like they were from another planet.

"So who said I would? Geez, Louise!' said Marsha. "Foster kids just make me a little nervous. I mean, the only foster kid I ever heard of was Heidi."

Collette shook her head. "Heidi who?"

"Heidi from the movie. You know, Shirley Temple played this sweet little kid who had to go live in the mountains with her mean old grandfather when her parents died. Then, he didn't want her for a long time and finally she was shipped off to be a foster kid with these rich people."

Mrs. Murphy reached out and tugged gently on Marsha's ponytail. "Well, *that* was a movie made in Hollywood, Marsha," she pointed out. "Mrs.

Lister's foster children used to live in the North Hills, not Switzerland. I don't think we will see anything so dramatic."

Collette bit her lip, feeling sorry already for the foster kids. They must miss their mother so much. She hated to think of how Laura, Jeff, and Stevie would feel if they were shipped away.

"Marsha, we have to treat these foster kids real special. I think they should win as many prizes as we can let them." Collette thought for a second. "But we can't be real obvious about it. Don't try to give them your old clothes or compliment them every five seconds."

"Marsha will be great with all the campers," said Mrs. Murphy.

"I'll try," Marsha said. "I wonder how long they'll last at the Listers' house. I baby-sat them last month and those boys are rough. They have crayon marks all over their walls and Mrs. Lister locks her bedroom door so they can't mess up her room. Those boys are so wild, their own cat ran away."

Everyone laughed. "I hope both foster kids are boys," said Collette. "They'll love being around Roger and John."

Mrs. Murphy grinned. "I know your brothers will be excited."

Collette felt a sudden chill. Her brothers? "Mom, this camp isn't for . . . for *brothers*. We want to keep it real professional, kind of 'no-relatives' allowed."

Mrs. Murphy looked up. "You mean your brothers and Laura aren't allowed to come to a camp being held in their own backyard?"

Collette could tell her mother was waiting for an answer. She probably wouldn't like the answer Collette wanted to give her.

"Collette, the little guys would be broken hearted if they thought you didn't want them at Camp Summer Fun."

"But, Mom . . ." Collette stopped. She had never even *considered* having her little brothers and sister in her camp. Including your whole family didn't sound one bit professional. Besides, all sorts of things could go wrong if they were there. First of all, they wouldn't listen to her; next they would show off and start wrestling in the middle of craft time and . . . Collette sighed. It just wouldn't work out.

Mrs. Murphy brushed back the damp hair from

Collette's forehead. "Collette, last night after you were asleep, Laura came downstairs carrying her piggy bank. She wanted me to break it so she could pay you herself. She said you could have every cent, even if it was too much."

"Oh Mom . . ." Collette hated it when her mother told her those corny, sentimental stories about her little brothers and sister. Her mother knew Collette would feel guilty. It was probably the worst mother trick of all because it always worked.

"Well . . . if I let them come to camp, will you talk to them and make them promise to listen to me?"

"And me," added Marsha quickly. "Remember, Collette. We are both the boss of this camp. Not just you."

Collette looked hopefully at Marsha. "Marsha's right. Since she is half boss, too, maybe she doesn't want them . . ."

Marsha grinned. "Hey, I don't care if they come. They can come as long as they pay. But, we better charge *double* for Stevie."

Collette frowned. It was easier for Marsha not to mind. After all, it wouldn't be *her* family ruining

Camp Summer Fun. What if Stevie turned the hose on everyone, just to make Jeff laugh? Or what if Laura followed Collette around like a shadow and refused to get in the story tent because it smelled like wet mud? Laura might tell everyone about the ten pound spider with hairy legs they discovered the last time they unfolded the tent. What if none of the campers would get into the tent?

Collette's heart started to beat faster. There could be lots of surprises at camp. What if all the campers started crying for their mothers at exactly the same time?

Collette felt her mother's cool hand on her neck. "Honey, give your brothers and Laura a chance. That's all I'm asking. If they act up, then I'll take them out myself. I promise."

Collette stood up. "Thanks, Mom." She leaned back and patted her mother's large middle. "Anyway, I guess it's better for them to be outside bugging me than inside bugging you and the baby."

Mrs. Murphy nodded. "Thanks. I better go call Mrs. Lister." She took one final look around the backyard. "This camp is going to be a lot of fun for everyone."

"Hey, hey, hey . . ." a voice called out. "This must be the famous camp the whole town is talking about." Roger Friday pulled off his sunglasses and wiggled his eyebrows at the girls as he strutted up the driveway. "We were able to switch our court time so we're all yours, ladies!"

Marsha nudged Collette with her elbow and sighed. "So much for prayers being answered."

Roger laughed. "Marsha, you prayed I would come? How sweet."

Collette and John started to laugh. Mrs. Murphy waved good-bye and started up the back stairs.

"What do you want us to do?" asked John.

"Do you know how to set up a tent?" Collette asked hopefully.

"Can a rooster crow?" asked Roger. "Can a bird fly?"

"Can *you* be quiet?" Marsha slapped her hand over her mouth and glanced quickly at John. Collette smiled. She knew Marsha was trying to stay as sweet as possible around John. With Roger here, it might be impossible.

"Let's check it out, Roger," said John. As he walked past Marsha, he grinned. "You can be the foreman, Marsha."

Roger walked by and slapped Marsha on the back. "Perfect job for the lady. There's nothing she likes better than telling people what to do. Right, sugar lips?"

Marsha swatted Roger and walked over to John. "Do you want me to hold your watch, John?"

Roger shook his head. "Hey, we're putting up a tent, not washing up for surgery, Marsha."

"Be quiet," hissed Marsha.

"Did you have any trouble switching courts?" asked Collette. She wanted to change the subject fast, before a fight could start. It was important to keep the chemistry working well through the whole week.

Roger shook his head. "Nah. I called a few people in a few high places and got it taken care of." Roger held one end of the tent while John pounded in a stake.

"I called, Rog," laughed John. He looked up at Collette. "I asked my cousin to trade court times with us. We practice at one o'clock now, instead of ten."

"Yeah," grumbled Rog. "I just hope I don't fry my brains out in that afternoon heat."

"No chance of that, Roger," Marsha said. "You have to *have* brains before you can fry them."

Collette looked at John. Was the war about to start? But John just laughed and started to pound in another stake. Marsha was busy holding up the center pole and Roger was zippering up the front screen door. They were working together beautifully.

"Great job, John!" Marsha said when the tent was up. She clapped and turned her back on Roger. "Now *John*, maybe you can help me with the horseshoe game."

"Hey, I *love* horseshoes," said Roger. "My gramps and I used to play them every Sunday when he lived on his farm."

Marsha barely glanced at Roger. "*John*, maybe you can help me carry over the water balloon buckets."

"Cool. I *love* water balloons," laughed Roger. "Where are they, Marsha?"

"Come and help me, Roger." Collette led the way into the garage. "Let's set up the croquet set first. My little brother loves hitting the balls around the yard."

"Your little brothers are cool," said Roger. "Will they be at the camp?"

"Yes," said Collette. She glanced over, wondering if Roger minded so many Murphys being in the camp. Stevie had ruined Open House in the third grade, and during the Christmas play he'd announced to the whole audience that he was going to throw up in two minutes. Maybe having Stevie Murphy in the camp was a little dangerous.

"Jeff can help me with a treasure hunt," said Roger. "We have one every Fourth of July at my Uncle Buck's. It's great."

"Jeff would love to help," said Collette. She felt better already. Maybe she was inventing things to worry about. Once her brothers realized how professional the camp was, maybe they would be too impressed to be rude. "Roger, let's set it up here."

Roger looked around the yard and frowned. "Are you sure you want the horseshoes this close to your house's windows? Some little kids can't aim too well. How about back by the brick wall?"

"Sounds good to me," Collette said. She hoped

Marsha had heard Roger's great suggestion. He already sounded like a real camp counselor.

"Hey Rog, as soon as you finish that, we better get going." John ran his hand through his sandy blond hair. "We can come back tomorrow and help some more." John looked around the yard. "It's going to be nice. I'm glad you girls asked us to help out."

Roger walked slowly around the yard, his hands shoved deep into his pockets. "Yeah sir, things are shaping up, ladies. I *like* what I see. What *the man* sees, he likes."

Collette smiled.

Marsha rolled her eyes. "Oh, brother."

Roger stared up at the sky, frowning at the gray clouds passing overhead. "But, we have to play it safe. We need some sort of shelter in case it rains. I think old Marsha here better get a broom and start sweeping the garage."

Marsha took a step closer to Roger. "Hey, the weather man promised sunshine every day, Mr. Friday. So don't go throwing your gloomy predictions around."

John and Roger exchanged looks. Roger tapped Marsha on the arm. "Well, in that case, sugar lips, why don't you just get on that broom and fly away?"

John was the first one to laugh. Collette smiled and then started to laugh, too. Finally, even Marsha smiled. It sounded great, all four counselors laughing together, just like real counselors in a movie. Collette looked across the yard, feeling good inside. Counting her own brothers and Laura, and the two foster kids, they now had fifteen kids signed up. Fifteen kids and four great counselors added up to one perfect summer camp week.

Chapter Four

Saturday, July 8th

Dear Sarah,

Hi. So, How's O-HI-O? Be careful you don't catch the bouquet at the wedding or you will be the next bride? (Ha, ha, snort, ha . . . anyone I know? Just kidding!!)

You'll never guess who is replacing you as a camp counselor . . . John McKechnie and Roger Friday. Of course it takes two boys to do the work of one fabulous girl. Marsha has been drooling over John. She

47

wore mascara this afternoon when the boys came back to set up the badminton net in our side yard. Then Roger threw a water balloon at Marsha. First, her mascara ran. Next, Marsha ran. After she washed her face she came back looking like the same old kid. She is sooooo funny!!!!!

I am really excited about camp. Marsha has lots of great ideas to get the kids warmed up. No one can be shy when she's in one of her great moods. She is giving half of her stuffed animal collection away as prizes. I saved the tiny pink rabbit for you . . . a welcome home present.

We have a total of fifteen kids. My two brothers, Laura, the new girl with red hair at the end of my block, the Cillo sisters, Tracey Jonas, some kid named Wilbur Platt, two girls from Morningside Avenue, a cute little boy named Petey and the Lister boys . . . plus . . . listen to this, Sarah. We are having two real foster kids! Mrs. Lister is taking care of *them because their mother is sick or something. My mom told me last night that the girl, Kicky, is already ten. I know that's kind of old for our camp, but she wants to stick close by her little brother, Eddie. He's only six. We will bend a rule or two since I feel so sorry for them. They must be soooooo sad!!!*

Wouldn't you just die if you had to be a foster kid and live with strangers? I told Marsha that we have to be extra, extra nice to them both. Our camp will probably be the best week of their whole sad summer. No matter what they do, I'm going to let them know I think they're terrific.

Well, I better go. I need my sleep so I can have lots of energy for camp. Not only do I have to entertain fifteen kids, but I have to make sure Roger and Marsha don't try to kill each other. (Only kidding . . . Marsha is trying to be sweet in front of John.)

I'll write you more tomorrow. Here's

a joke to keep you laughing until then:

Why'd the chicken fall out of the tree?
He fainted.

Why'd the monkey fall out of the tree?
He was stapled to the chicken . . . ha,
ha, heh!!!!

> *Love,*
> *Your Best Friend,*
> *Collette*

> *Sunday, July 9th*

Dear Sarah,

I know you are thrilled to be getting
two letters in a row from me. I am writ-
ing this in the bathroom because it is
already ten o'clock and Laura is asleep
and I am supposed to be, too. Tomorrow
is the biggggg day. I am so excited and
so nervous, all rolled up into one big fraz-
zled ball. Marsha made me look at all the
new shorts she is going to wear this
week. She is trying to get John Mc-

Kechnie to fall in love with her. Ha. I don't want to hurt her feelings but John is more interested in winning an August tennis tournament. Roger is a riot. He has been real helpful. He even made a big welcome sign for the garage door. Boy he's a good artist. I hope I say the right things to the foster kids. I want this week to be special for them. Laura wrapped up her favorite bracelet in a sandwich bag and she is going to give it to the foster girl. Laura is so sweet. I hope my mom has another girl, even if she has to sleep in the bedroom with us. I'll still love the baby, even if it's a boy, but what if it turns out to be another Stevie? He hid his chewing gum in Jeff's mashed potatoes tonight and didn't tell Jeff till he had eaten every last spoonful. Boy was my dad mad!!!!! He made Stevie go to bed right after dinner. Now Jeff thinks the gum will start blowing up inside his stomach tonight. Ha. Little kids are sooooo strange.

Well, take care of yourself, Sarah.

John gave me an extra shirt for you.
"Lucky Strikers" is printed on the front.
We can all wear them next year in seventh grade. People will think we're related to John.

Wish me luck. I am so excited!

> Worried, but excited, and
> still your best friend,
> Collette

Chapter Five

On Monday morning, Collette was up, dressed in her red "Lucky Strikers" shirt, and downstairs by seven-thirty. She was so excited about the first day of camp, she could barely finish breakfast. She turned the knob of the radio until she heard the weather. "Wow! Mom, did you hear that? It's going to be eighty-one degrees today." Collette ran to the window again to see if any campers had arrived early for their first day. "I hope everyone remembers that camp starts *today*."

"Collette, calm down." Mr. Murphy laughed. "It's only seven-thirty. No one is going to be this early." He grabbed his suit jacket off the back of the chair. "I want to hear all about camp as soon as I get home."

Collette hugged her father. "Okay. Daddy, you did have a talk with the boys, right? Did you tell them they weren't allowed to be rude?"

"Yes. Jeff and Stevie said they would help you and Laura said she will call you Miss Murphy so you will feel like a real teacher."

"A *counselor*, Daddy." Collette smoothed out her red shirt. It had a large white bowling ball in the center. Collette and Marsha had used glitter pens to print the counselors' names above the bowling ball. The shirts looked great!

Mrs. Murphy set her juice glass in the sink and kissed Collette and Mr. Murphy. "I better go help Stevie find Jeff's old cowboy boots. He woke up last night at two in the morning to look for them."

Mr. Murphy laughed. "Well, you seem to be getting up every hour to go to the bathroom, anyway. That baby is strong. He kicked me right out of bed during the middle of the night."

"Very funny." Mrs. Murphy winked at Collette. "I'm the only one getting up. Your father sleeps like a rock, Collette."

Collette grinned and followed her mother to the

hall. "Daddy promised to change at least three diapers a day with this baby, Mom." Collette could hear stomping upstairs. It had to be Stevie, getting ready for camp. "Mom, can you please make Stevie wear his tennis shoes? I don't want him looking weird in front of my campers. And remind them all that I'm in charge. They have to do what I say."

"Talk to your father," said Mrs. Murphy as she walked down the hall. "He said he was going to handle everything."

Collette's father picked up his briefcase. "I promised Stevie I would pay him fifty cents to be good for you. I told him to be a helper."

Collette gave her father a weak smile. He was trying to help. Too bad he didn't want to take Stevie to work with him for the next week. That would be a *real* help.

"Stevie picked his job," began Mr. Murphy, starting to smile. "He said he would be the spider-stepper man. When ever you need a spider stepped on, he'll be your man. He told me all camps have spiders."

"But he looks so *weird* in those boots, Dad."

Mr. Murphy checked his watch and kissed Collette. "He'll be okay, honey. Besides, his job will keep him busy and out of your mother's way. See you tonight, Peanut. Help Mom as much as you can."

Collette went back to the window. Stevie was still clomping around upstairs.

"Is anybody here yet?" Laura hurried into the kitchen, her arms filled with coloring books and crayons. A teddy bear, tied with a piece of frayed red ribbon, dragged along behind her.

"No. Laura, what are you doing with all that junk?"

Laura looked up, her round green eyes starting to fill with tears. "This isn't *junk*, Collette. This is stuff to cheer up any crying little kid who doesn't want to come to your camp but his mommy is making him come anyway."

Collette walked closer to Laura's pile.

"See?" Laura held up a coloring book. "I have lots of pages that Stevie didn't scribble on yet." Laura held up her worn-looking bear. "And I put a string on my bear so we could hang him from a tree like Tarzan. And, best of all," Laura held up the plastic baggie with her favorite pink bracelet. "I can hardly wait to give it to the poor girl living with Mrs. Lister."

"Laura, Kicky isn't poor. Her mom is just sick right now."

Laura frowned. "But she'll still need my bracelet, right?"

Collette smiled. "Sure. You're so nice, Laura."

"Thanks, Collette. You're nice, too."

It *had* been sweet of Laura to lug all her treasures downstairs. Collette didn't want to hurt her feelings by telling her that none of the campers would need cheering up. All the campers would be happy to be part of Camp Summer Fun. Collette stopped. But what about the foster kids? Maybe they *would* need cheering up. Maybe Laura could turn out to be a real help after all.

"Thanks, Laura. Maybe we could keep all your junk . . . I mean, *treasures*, in the garage."

Laura frowned. "No, Collette. There are spiders in the garage. They live in little dusty spider houses by the hose, Stevie said. He said it's their fort. They have little spider guns made from grass."

Collette tried to swallow a groan. Stevie and his

57

wild imagination was going to cause *some* sort of trouble, she just knew it. Too bad they didn't have a summer camp nearby to send Stevie to.

"Laura, I'll set you up by the door, in the sunshine," said Collette quickly. "You can be the camp nurse. If anyone gets sad, I can send him in to see you and you can cheer him up."

"Wow!" Laura wrapped her arms around Collette's waist. "Thanks, Collette. I would love to be the cheer-up lady. Can I wear a white dress and white shoes?"

Collette glanced down at her sister's flowered T-shirt and green shorts. Laura looked pretty cute right now. Collette didn't want her whole family looking like a bunch of weirdos.

"Just ask Jeff if you can wear his white baseball hat, Laura. Nurses try to stay cool in the summer, so they can think faster."

Laura nodded. "Okay. But I'll go change my socks. Nurses always wear white socks. When Mommy brings the new baby home, I'm going to wear white socks every day so I can be a baby nurse."

As soon as Laura ran back upstairs, Jeff walked

into the living room. He looked mad. "I don't want to be in your dumb camp, Collette. I'm almost ten. Tell Mom I don't have to, okay?"

"It isn't dumb. Besides, Dad said not to bother Mom. You don't have to make clay dishes or macaroni necklaces. You'll be more of a helper. I'll pay you five bucks for the week, okay?"

Jeff smiled. "Hey, okay. Dad already promised to pay me four. Maybe your camp won't be so dumb after all. I'm getting rich."

Collette couldn't help but feel a little insulted. Her camp was *not* dumb. Nobody should have to be paid just to show up.

Collette followed Jeff to the window. "Just remember, I am the boss of my camp, Jeff. It's a rule."

"Hey, open up, somebody!" Marsha stood in the back doorway holding an armful of squirt guns.

"Marsha, what do you have?" Collette laughed as she opened the screen door and picked up one of the squirt guns from Marsha. "What are these for?"

Marsha giggled. "I thought we could hide in the bushes and squirt the kids when they came

59

up your driveway. I won't squirt the foster kids, of course, but the other kids will think it's real funny."

Collette shook her head. "Marsha, I don't think we want to scare the little kids. Besides, parents will be happier if they think we *aren't* crazy."

Marsha dropped her squirt guns onto the kitchen table. "Well, maybe you're right. Jeff, why don't we fill up a few and chase Stevie." Marsha went to the sink and then turned back to Collette. "Just because I let you change my mind about the squirt guns, Collette, don't think you get to be the only one in charge. Remember, we *both* make up the rules."

Collette nodded. "I know. Just get this shoot-out over with before camp starts. Roger said he and John will be here at eight-forty-five."

Marsha shuddered. "I was hoping Roger forgot camp started today."

"I'll go get the name tags," said Collette. "I think the campers should wear their tags for the first day or two until we learn their names."

"Okay. And my mom is bringing over some more stuff for the craft table. She is going to bring some knitting and sit over there under the tree in

60

case we need her. If your mom feels okay, she can be in charge tomorrow." Marsha shoved a loaded squirt gun down the waistband of her shorts. "Too bad Sarah is going to miss all this fun."

"Yeah, I know . . ."

"Hey, Collette. Look at me!" Stevie raced into the kitchen. He was wearing Jeff's huge cowboy boots and had a large beach towel pinned to his shirt. Swim goggles rested atop his blond curls.

"Holy moley, what is he supposed to be?" asked Marsha. She started to laugh. "Cosmic Camper!"

"Stevie, do you really have to wear all that?" asked Collette. "I mean, I think you could run faster in your own tennis shoes."

Stevie put his hands on his hips and started marching around the kitchen table. "All spider-smasher guys wear this stuff. And I have to wear these goggles in case I step on a real fat spider and his guts splash up on my face."

"Oh, gross," mumbled Collette. How could she talk Stevie out of his job? Maybe she could pay him a dollar a day to just stay upstairs and play with his G.I. Joes.

Marsha pulled out her gun and squirted Stevie. "Hey, watch out for my spider poison, Stevie!"

Stevie let out a loud whoop and charged toward Marsha. Marsha tossed Jeff a loaded squirt gun and bolted out the back door.

Collette followed Jeff and Stevie out the back door and into the yard. Stevie snapped his goggles over his eyes and gave a loud whoop before he charged through the hedges after Jeff and Marsha.

"Is somebody crying?" Laura hurried down the driveway with a coloring book in one hand and her plastic stethoscope in the other. She was wearing white socks and Collette's white dress-up heels. "Collette, does someone need me yet?"

As Marsha, Jeff and Stevie sped past and down the street, Collette sat down on the milk box. She was the only counselor who was ready for duty.

"Roll out the carpet, start the band . . . we are here!"

Collette stood as Roger and John rode up the driveway on their bikes. Great! Now she would be able to get organized. Jeff would stop complaining so the older boys would think he was cool and Marsha would behave because John was here.

"Where should we leave our bikes?" asked John.

"Behind the garage, by the fence," Collette said. She felt another rush of excitement. Camp was about to begin. Everything was ready. The welcome banner was stretched out across the garage, and both boys were wearing their red shirts.

"Be right back, Collette," John called out. He turned and grinned. "I have this great game all planned."

Just then Stevie raced through the hedge, his beach towel flapping in the breeze. Marsha and Jeff chased after him, their squirt guns blasting. Stevie turned and tossed a tennis ball at Marsha, firing as he galloped across the yard and onto the driveway, right in front of John's bike.

"Hey, look out!" John yanked back hard on his handle bars, spinning his bike around.

"Help!" screamed Stevie, covering his head with both hands. "Wipe out!!"

Roger's bike swerved to avoid Stevie and smashed into John. Before Collette could even move, both boys were in a heap of spinning bike wheels and twisted arms and legs.

Chapter Six

John lay on the driveway, twisting in pain. "Oh, my leg," he muttered. "I think I broke my leg!"

"Oh-my-gosh-oh-my-gosh! It's all my fault!" sobbed Marsha. She threw her squirt gun in the grass and knelt beside John. "I'm so sorry, John. I didn't even know you were here. I was chasing Stevie. I . . . I didn't even see you."

"Oh, man . . ." John shook his head and his leg buckled under him. "It hurts too much."

"Jeff, tell Mom to get out here right away!" yelled Collette. She looked at the blood on John's forehead and knees. That didn't look too bad. But his right leg was turned so far to the left it looked like someone had tried to twist it off.

"Drag that milk box over here, Marsha!" ordered Roger. Collette was glad that Roger had escaped with only a skinned arm and leg. He must have fallen on John first and then bounced off.

"Let me do it, Roger," begged Laura. "I'm the nurse lady."

By the time Mrs. Murphy hurried out, John was sitting on the milk carton in the middle of the driveway with a bleached white face and a shin that was turning purple.

"It's all my fault," repeated Marsha, softer now.

"You sure took a spill, John," said Collette.

"I'm sure it was an accident. Marsha, run in and get some ice. I'm going to call John's mother." Mrs. Murphy went back inside.

"I'll get the bikes out of the way," offered Jeff.

Marsha hopped down the back stairs and rushed over, handing John a large plastic baggie filled with ice. "Do you want some water, John?" asked Marsha. "Or I could run home and make you some lemonade. Fresh. It wouldn't take long. I wouldn't mind."

"No . . ." John bit down hard on his lip.

"Sorry, John," said Stevie. "I didn't see you. I'm sorry you got hurt."

John just nodded. "I'm okay," he said softly. But he sure didn't look okay. By the time his mother and older sisters arrived, his face was whiter than Collette's clipboard sheet.

"Call us from the hospital," said Mrs. Murphy, putting her hand on Marsha's shoulder as Mrs. McKechnie's station wagon backed slowly out of the driveway.

"Here's our first customer," announced Roger as the very first camper started up the driveway.

Marsha covered her face and turned around. "John probably hates me," she sobbed.

"No, he doesn't. It's time to start the camp, Marsha. Smile, it was an accident." Collette put her arm around her.

"Yeah," sniffed Marsha. "Caused by me."

"Uh-oh, here comes your first camper," said Mrs. Murphy. "Good morning! Welcome to camp!" Collette knew her mother was using her loudest, most cheerful voice to boost everyone's spirits. "Hello, Wilbur. Good morning, Mrs. Platt. Wait till you see the backyard. It looks great."

Collette watched how smoothly her mother walked down to greet the little boy. Mrs. Murphy talked a mile a minute, laughing and telling Wilbur all about the crafts and snacks waiting for him. "You are going to have so much fun today."

"I'll go play with Wilbur," offered Roger. "You two reel in the next kid. He's getting out of that white car."

Roger grabbed a basketball from the basket and started bouncing it across the driveway. "Hey, my name's Roger, Wilbur. How about a little one-on-one, buddy?"

"I'm going home," Marsha declared. She wiped her smeared face with the sleeve of her T-shirt. "I'm sorry, Collette, but I don't want to be a counselor anymore."

"What?" Collette grabbed Marsha's arm as she walked past. "You *can't* quit, Marsha!"

Marsha drew in a deep breath and closed her eyes. "I have to quit. I feel too *guilty* to be a camp counselor, Collette. I want to go home and be alone."

Collette blocked Marsha's path. "But . . . but you can't. In five minutes we are going to be *surrounded* by little kids and you have to stay here and help."

Marsha shoved her hands on her hips. "You're not the boss of me, Collette, so stop giving me orders. Just because we're using your backyard, you think you are the biggest boss, but you aren't."

"Marsha, you can't just . . ."

"Hello . . . hello!"

Mrs. Lister and her boys started up the driveway.

"Hi, Collette!" shouted Matt. "I'm here! Do you have any pretzels? Where's Stevie?"

"Hi. Yes, and Stevie's somewhere . . ." Collette smiled, keeping one eye on Marsha to make sure she wasn't going to sneak down the driveway. Following behind Mrs. Lister was a girl as tall as Collette. She was holding onto a little boy who looked a lot like Stevie. Instead of Stevie's blond curls, this little boy had brown curly hair and reddish freckles sprinkled across his cheeks like cinnamon.

"The foster kids are here, Marsha," announced Collette.

Marsha shrugged, then whispered. "Collette, I am too upset to be extra nice to those kids. I feel sorry for them, too, since they have such a crummy life, but maybe your mom could help out . . ."

Collette gripped Marsha's wrist and squeezed

68

it. "Don't you *dare* try to leave, Marsha," she hissed.

Matt and Mikey raced past Collette and Marsha.

"Roger," called out Collette. "Grab two name tags and stick them on the Lister boys."

"If you can catch them," laughed Mrs. Lister. She smiled at Collette. "Here at last."

"Hi," Collette said cheerfully. Out of the corner of her eye, she could see two little girls climbing down from an orange van marked MORNINGSIDE DAY CARE. Collette was glad to see how cheerfully her mother greeted them both. Laura was following a man who held his crying daughter. Laura was holding up a coloring book and cracker to the little girl.

"Please stop crying," Laura kept saying. Collette recognized them as the new family that had just moved to the street behind the Murphys.

"Don't make me stay, Daddy!" wailed the little girl. The man tried to put her down, but his daughter only clung more tightly to his neck, dangling like a huge pendant.

"So how is the first day going?" asked Mrs. Lister.

"Fine. Welcome to Camp Summer Fun!" Collette sang out. She tried to sound as cheerful as her mother had.

"Hello, Collette and Marsha. I want you to meet Kicky and her brother, Eddie. They are staying with my family," explained Mrs. Lister.

"Hi," said Marsha. She took a step down the driveway and Collette grabbed the back of her shirt. There was no way Marsha was going to try and sneak away.

Collette knew once camp started going, Marsha would forget all about going home. She was great with little kids.

"Hi, Eddie. Hi, Kicky!" Collette put her hand on Eddie's shoulder. "My little brother Stevie is over there by the sandbox. He's five."

Eddie's eyes flashed. "I was five *last* year."

"Thanks for coming to our camp," said Collette.

Kicky looked around the backyard. "Is this the *whole* camp?"

Collette nodded. The backyard was filled with picnic tables, sandboxes, wading pools, two craft tables, and a huge storytelling tent. It looked great.

Kicky crossed her arms and raised her eyebrows. "This isn't a camp. It looks like a play group." She turned to Mrs. Lister. "I thought you said I would enjoy this."

Collette's and Mrs. Lister's cheeks flushed red at the same time.

"We have a lot of things planned," said Collette quickly. "*Fun* things."

"But, if you think ten years old is too grown-up for this camp, you can come on back to the house with me," offered Mrs. Lister. "Why, I would love to take you up to the new mall, or maybe a little walk around North Park Lake. It would be fun to have girl time."

Eddie reached up and grabbed onto Kicky's hand. "Don't go, Kicky. Stay with me."

Kicky shook her head and squeezed her little brother's hand. "Thanks, Mrs. Lister, but I've got to watch out for Eddie."

Eddie grinned at everyone. "Once Kicky went to a camp that had a hundred horses. Even an all-white horse named King, right, Kicky?"

Kicky smiled at her brother. "His name was General."

Eddie nodded. "Yeah, and when Mommy comes back, she is going to take us to that camp, too, to meet General."

Collette nodded. She slid a glance over at Kicky, wondering if she really went to that fancy camp, or if she was just making up stories for Eddie.

"I better get name tags on all the kids," said Marsha. She dug into her shorts and pulled out a purple marker.

"Here guys, print your name." Marsha handed Eddie and Kicky a small white square.

Kicky knelt down and neatly printed Eddie's name. She peeled off the backing and carefully stuck it to his shirt. Then she stood up and handed back her tag. "Here, I don't want to wear one."

"You have to," said Marsha, handing it back. "It's a camp rule."

Kicky just shrugged and ignored the tag. "I already know who I am."

"But all the campers . . ." Marsha began.

"I think it's okay if Kicky doesn't wear one," said Collette quickly. She grinned at Kicky. "Hey, no big deal."

Mrs. Lister broke into a smile. "Well, I'll be back around twelve then." She put her hand on Kicky's arm. "If you need me, dear, just give me a call. Do you have the number?"

Kicky nodded. She even smiled at Mrs. Lister. "Yeah. We'll be okay."

"*Everyone* will be okay, Mrs. Lister," said Collette in an extra cheerful voice. "See you at noon."

As soon as Mrs. Lister headed down the driveway, Collette grabbed her clipboard. "Kicky, I'm going to check off the campers now. Would you like to help?"

Kicky shook her head. "No. I don't know these kids."

"Oh, well, I just thought . . ." Collette smiled again. "If you want, you can go inside and get some cold lemonade."

Kicky shook her head again and turned away. "What do you want to do, Eddie?"

"Play," said Eddie. "But you come and watch me, okay, Kicky?"

Collette hurried down to the end of the driveway to help her mom. The sad little girl was sitting on the bench, coloring with Laura.

"Hi, guys!" said Collette. "I'm a counselor."

"That's my sister, Collette." Laura leaned over and hugged the little girl. "And this is Karen and I made her stop crying all by myself."

"You are a great cheer-up lady, Laura. Hi, Karen!" Collette stuck a name tag on both of them and started back up to the yard. Twelve of the campers were already there. As soon as the other three arrived, she would call roll and start with a song.

Collette glanced across the yard at Kicky. She was leaning against the stone wall, watching Eddie in the sandbox. Too bad she couldn't send Laura over to put a smile on Kicky's face. Why was Kicky so angry? Maybe she didn't like the idea of camp. Or maybe she was upset because her mom was sick.

By the time the last camper had arrived, the backyard was noisy. Roger was lining up a group to toss baskets and Marsha was unscrewing bottles of poster paint.

"Come on, guys," called out Collette. She gave two blasts on her whistle. "Time to start some fun! Who wants to learn some songs and toss some water balloons?"

Eddie broke away from Kicky and came running over. "Collette, wait. I have to tell you something. My sister and I can't get our clothes dirty."

He patted his yellow T-shirt. "These are brand, brand new."

"Oh, you won't get too dirty, Eddie," promised Collette. "Mostly wet. Mrs. Lister can wash your clothes. She bought them for you because she wants you to enjoy them."

"Our *mother* bought us these clothes," said Kicky as she walked up from behind. "And we have a whole closet full at home."

Eddie nodded. "But we don't want to get all dirty."

Collette nodded. "Fine. Well, you guys can do whatever you want. I mean, if you want to just watch, that's okay with me."

Kicky nodded back. "That's right."

Roger ran up and tossed the ball to Eddie. "Hey, come on over, my man. Let's see what kind of shooter you are." Roger pointed his finger at Kicky. "Hey, you better get a name tag. We're just about to start."

"Oh, that's okay," interrupted Collette quickly. "I think we'll remember Kicky's name." Collette smiled at the girl. "I love your name," Collette said. "Is Kicky short for Katherine?"

"No," said Kicky. She didn't offer anymore.

Eddie tugged on Collette's shirt. "We call her Kicky cause she likes to kick."

Kicky looked up then, giving Collette a slow smile. She looked proud.

"Whatever," muttered Roger. "I'll line up the kids so they can introduce themselves."

"Whoopee dee doo," said Kicky in a flat voice.

"Sounds good, Roger!" Collette tried to sound upbeat. She even grinned at Kicky. But Kicky just looked through Collette as if she was a window, and after a few seconds, Collette's own smile felt plastic.

Chapter Seven

"Whoa — something is definitely wrong with that Kicky person, Collette." Marsha bent down and turned on the hose, rinsing her hands. "That girl has got a *real* problem."

"Shhhhhhh . . . Of course she does. She's a foster kid," whispered Collette. "You promised to be nice to her."

"Nice?" Marsha's voice rose. "Collette, I have a *splitting headache* from trying so hard to be nice to Kicky. But it's impossible to get anything out of her. She refused to say anything during the introduction period, and when I asked her if she wanted to make a macaroni necklace to take to her mom in the hospital, or wherever she is, she told me to drop dead. Boy, oh, boy, that foster kid isn't one bit like Heidi. In the movie, Heidi was cheerful and always trying to help people and . . ."

"Well, keep trying. Come on, we've got to get back to work." Collette hugged her clipboard and hurried over to help Roger. He had the volume all the way up on his tape deck, blasting Christmas music over the entire camp.

"Do you need any help, Santa man?" asked Collette.

"Sure do," said Roger, fluffing up his beard. "Reach in my sack and pass out some peppermint sticks and then help me load up my sleigh."

"Me, first!" cried Eddie. He stuck his peppermint stick in his shirt pocket and held out his arms. Roger swung him up in the air and placed him in the red wagon.

"All aboard for the North Pole!" Roger called out.

"I want a ride," cried Tracey.

Collette handed Tracey a peppermint stick and Roger swung her into the wagon next. Collette giggled, watching Roger pull the kids up and down the driveway, everyone singing along with the tape. Keeping kids entertained wasn't so hard. They liked to do everything.

"Don't let that peppermint stick melt through your good shirt, Eddie," called out Kicky from under the shade tree.

Eddie pulled it out and handed it to Roger who put it in his own shirt. Collette stole a glance at Kicky. Marsha was right. Kicky hadn't even tried to join in all morning. Her only purpose at the camp was to make sure Eddie was okay.

Collette glanced over her shoulder at Stevie and Laura. Both of them were playing croquet with Marsha's mother. Jeff was struggling to carry down the heavy cooler from the kitchen. Collette thought she was a pretty good big sister, but Kicky made her look like she didn't do much at all. Kicky acted like a twenty-four-hour guardian angel.

When Eddie's turn was over, he continued to follow Roger up and down the driveway, refusing to do anything else except be Roger's shadow.

After all the peppermint sticks were passed out and the rest of the line had a ride in Roger's sleigh, Collette went over to help Marsha start the face painting.

"Roger is so funny," said Collette. She stood

beside Marsha, watching as she whipped together another batch of vanilla pudding for the face painting. Marsha loved the idea that the kids could lick off their design.

"Funny as in ha-ha, or funny as in odd?" asked Marsha as she squirted red food coloring into the pudding. "He's doing an all right job, I guess."

"Are you ready for the kids?" asked Collette. She glanced down at her watch. It was already ten-fifteen and she wanted to keep things on schedule.

Marsha laid down her spoon and nodded. "Yes, sir. Get those kids over here." Marsha pointed to a red heart on her own cheek. "I'm advertising our blue star special . . . a red heart." Marsha picked up her paintbrush and grinned at Collette. "In fact, I think I'll choose my first victim."

Marsha crossed the yard and walked over to Kicky. She grinned and waved her paintbrush up and down like a cigar. "Hey there, Kecky, want me to paint your face?"

Collette saw Kicky's back straighten.

"It's *Kicky*, Marsha," corrected Collette. Collette hadn't had a chance to tell Marsha what the

Kicky stood for. Maybe it was better she didn't know.

Marsha shrugged. "Kick, Keck, what's the difference?" Marsha laughed.

Kicky frowned at Marsha. "I guess there's no difference between Marsha and Marsh-mellow."

Marsha's cheeks grew pink, but she smiled back. "Yeah, I guess I see what you mean. Sorry, Kicky. So anyway, do you want me to paint your face?"

Kicky shook her head. "No."

"You can lick off the design if you don't like it," added Marsha. "The paint is made from pudding."

"I said no," Kicky said shortly. She stood up and brushed past Marsha. "I've got a *splitting headache.*"

Collette's heart leaped. Her eyes met Marsha's and both girls blushed deep red. Kicky must have heard! Collette gripped her clipboard, trying to remember exactly what they had said.

Collette cleared her throat and tried to smile. "Your little brother sure likes Roger, Kicky."

"Eddie likes everyone," said Kicky. She drew in a deep breath and let it out. "I don't."

"Sure you do, Kicky," Collette said automatically.

"No, I don't," repeated Kicky.

Collette opened her mouth, then closed it. She wanted to tell Kicky to at least try and like everyone. She would have said it in a second to Stevie, Laura, or any of the other campers.

But maybe some foster kids were too sad to be friendly. Especially Kicky.

"Is camp almost over?" Kicky asked in a bored voice.

Collette felt Marsha's elbow in her back, but she didn't turn around. She could tell Marsha's temper was about to heat up.

"It has been a long morning," agreed Collette. She glanced around at the other campers, each of whom seemed to be having fun. Didn't Kicky notice that? Couldn't she hear Eddie and Stevie laughing?

"I see I have a line forming for face painting," Marsha said quickly. "See you later."

"Hey," Collette said brightly. "It's snacktime, Kicky. I was just getting ready to pass out some Popsicles." Collette walked over and lifted the lid of the huge red cooler. "We have grape or lemon. Would you like to help?"

"Isn't that what *you're* getting paid for?"

Collette opened her mouth, then clamped it shut again. "That's all right. My mom said she wanted to help pass them out so she could check up on Stevie, Jeff, and Laura. To make sure they aren't getting in the way."

"Is your mom the pregnant one?" asked Kicky.

Collette nodded. "Yes. The baby's due in a few more weeks. We're so excited."

"Then why don't you let her sit down and *you* pass out your own Popsicles?"

"Well . . ." Collette wasn't quite sure what to say. Maybe Kicky's own mother was pregnant and having problems. Maybe that's why she had to let Kicky and Eddie become foster kids.

"Marsha has her mother helping with the craft table, too," pointed out Kicky. "Don't you think you girls are a little *old* to still need your mother's help?"

Collette nodded, then shook her head. "Well, no, because we have to have an adult near by since we're only eleven. It's some sort of law."

Kicky laughed. But it wasn't a friendly laugh. "Oh, yeah. Well, I've been taking care of Eddie since I was six. I guess the police in our neighborhood didn't read their rule book."

"Since you were six?" Collette cried. "That's so young."

"Says who?"

Collette leaned closer, waiting for Kicky to finish. But Kicky just stopped, clamping down hard on the rest of her sentence.

Collette picked up the cooler and stole another look at Kicky, wondering if it would help or hurt to ask a question about her mother. Like what was wrong with her? Was she in the hospital? When would she be well enough to come and take Kicky and Eddie back home?

The deep frown on Kicky's face let Collette know that now wasn't a good time to ask her anything.

"I'm going to go pass these out," said Collette.

"Oh, brother. I might as well help," sighed Kicky. "So you won't have to bother your mom."

"Great, thanks," said Collette. Kicky took one end of the cooler and the two traveled around the yard, passing out freezer pops and sticking the wrappers in a trash bag. When they got to Eddie, Kicky shook her head.

"Don't take one, Eddie. You're gonna drip all over your new shirt. Mrs. Lister will get mad."

Collette saw the disappointed look on Eddie's face. He put both hands behind his back and nodded at his sister.

"Hey, it's only colored water, Kicky," laughed Collette. "Besides, it washes right out. Stevie is always dripping all over himself."

Kicky dropped the freezer pops back into the cooler and took Eddie's hand. "You leave Eddie to me, okay?"

"Hey, I'm going to have one," said Roger. "It might cool you off, partner." Roger stuck his hand in the cooler and chose an orange pop. He sprinkled icy drops of water on Eddie and laughed. Eddie smiled back.

"Eddie, your face is as red as an apple," said Kicky gently. "Let's sit in the shade for a few minutes."

Collette watched as the two of them walked away.

"Whoa, what's wrong with that girl?" asked Roger. "I haven't seen her smile all morning." He nudged Collette with his elbow. "And we all know the magic I can work with most women."

Collette grinned. "The kids all seem to like you a lot, Roger. I don't know about Kicky. I don't think she likes anyone except Eddie. Maybe she's just shy."

Roger shrugged. "I don't think that's it. I told her I was sorry to hear her mother was sick and she told me to shut up and mind my own business." Roger pointed his freezer pop at Collette. "Shy people don't talk that way. She acts a little too much like Marsha for my blood."

Marsha hurried over and pulled out a freezer pop. "Whoa, am I glad my mom is here. She's making some more pudding for the face painting." Marsha tore off the wrapper and took a big bite. "Boy, am I ever tired. I think fifteen kids are ten too many." She chewed quickly. "My mom said John's mom called. The good news is John didn't break anything, but the bad news is he has to stay off his leg for three or four days."

"Good. We'll still be able to play our tennis match," said Roger. "I'll call him tonight."

"I'll call him, too," said Marsha. "I hope he's not mad at me."

86

"He's not," Collette said quickly.

Roger looked around the yard. "I'll help Jeff finish up the horseshoe game with those kids." Roger pointed his finger at Marsha. "Collette, don't let Marsha take more than a five-minute break."

"Why don't you take five minutes and go break your neck, Roger," laughed Marsha. She stuck out a purple tongue.

Collette noticed Kicky look up. She scowled at Marsha and then continued raking her fingers through the grass.

"Marsha, don't insult Roger like that in front of the campers. It isn't *professional*," Collette said.

Marsha licked off her fingers and giggled. "Yeah, well, Roger isn't human, so what else is new?"

Collette picked up the cooler and headed toward the sandbox. The little Cillo girls would love a Popsicle. Their mom always dressed them so cute, but she never minded how dirty they got. "Kids are supposed to get dirty," Mrs. Cillo always said. Collette walked past Kicky. She wondered if Kicky had ever been a kid.

Chapter Eight

"Please tell me it's noon already," groaned Marsha. "I've made three gallons of face paint, twenty-seven million macaroni necklaces, and played at least five games of Simon Says."

"And the kids are having so much fun," said Collette proudly. Marsha had been terrific with the kids all morning. "Okay, Marsha, let's see what's on the schedule next." Collette pushed back her damp hair. It was so hot. "It's almost eleven-thirty, so I'll get the group together for a quick story by the tent." Collette nudged Marsha. "It's too hot to put the kids in the tent today."

"You could let them play follow-the-leader

through the sprinkler before storytime," suggested Marsha. "It will cool the kids off."

"Great idea!" Collette scribbled Marsha's suggestion on top of storytime.

"Of course it's a great idea, dar-ling," laughed Marsha. "It came from me, didn't it?"

"Storytime by the tent, kids!" called out Collette. She put her hand in front of her mouth and whispered. "I bet Kicky won't let Eddie walk through the sprinkler."

"Probably not. She won't let him get wet, dirty or hot. Hey, Collette, make sure your storytime is finished by eleven-fifty at the very latest because I have a very special announcement about tomorrow and I want to explain it to the kids."

Collette glanced down at the clipboard. "You'll have to do it tomorrow, Marsha. Roger has a water balloon toss planned for eleven-fifty. Then camp will be over for the day."

Marsha sighed. "Well, tell Roger to let me talk to the kids real fast first. I need time to explain my project before the parents come to pick up their kids."

"But the kids need time to dry off before the

parents pick them up, Marsha. Roger wrote *his* time in first."

Marsha wiped her hands on her shorts. "Can you ask Roger to switch times with me, Collette? After all, you and I are the main people in charge here. I'm practically head counselor since I'm two months older than you. Believe me, my contest is going to be the hit of the whole week."

"Collette!" Mrs. Cessano waved her sun hat at the girls. "The storytime group is ready, dear."

"Talk to Roger for me, okay? There won't be any time left to explain about my contest. Pleeeeeaaaasssssssse, Collette."

"No, Roger is all ready. It isn't fair, Marsha," began Collette.

"Oh, forget it. I'll go turn on the sprinkler." Marsha gave one final scowl and marched off.

Collette rubbed her forehead. Too bad Sarah wasn't here. She could have teased Marsha back into a better mood.

Collette hurried over to the campers. Most of them looked very hot. "Storytime will start in just a few minutes, guys," explained Collette. "But if you're real hot, you can run through the sprinkler in the side yard. Run through four times and then come right back."

"Can I run through seven times, Collette?" asked Stevie. His blond curls were soaked with sand and sweat. "I'm real hot and Jeff says I stink."

"*Four* times, Stevie," Collette said firmly. "You have to follow the rules."

While Collette waited for her group, she leaned back against the tree. She had been too rushed even to ask Marsha more about her contest. It was probably a great idea, but it would be just as great tomorrow. Marsha had to learn to follow the rules, just like Stevie.

"Hey!" Collette looked up and saw Roger looking down at her. "You better hurry with your story because I have all my balloons ready. I don't want the kids dripping wet when their parents pick them up."

"Okay." Collette stood up and blasted her whistle. "Turn off the sprinkler, Marsha. Come on, campers. Storytime."

Marsha must have said something funny because the kids all started laughing and clapping.

Roger laughed. "Marsha drives me nuts, but she is pretty good with kids, isn't she?"

"Yeah," agreed Collette. "She's a little mad at me right now. She wanted me to ask you to switch activity times with her. She wants to explain about a contest."

"Tell her I said no. Who elected Marsha our fearless leader?" laughed Roger. "Face it, Collette. We are the only people in the world who say no to that kid."

Collette nodded and grinned. "She can't help it she's rich, and an only child, and . . ."

"And spoiled rotten." Roger leaned over and studied the clipboard. "So what is her contest about, anyway?"

Collette shrugged. "We'll have to wait till to-morrow."

Collette blasted her whistle. "Storytime. Run to the tent, kids."

As the kids flopped down on the blanket outside the tent, Roger turned and left.

Collette picked up her book and sat down on the blanket. Collette opened the large book and started to read, her voice carrying across the small heads in front of her.

"Once upon a time," began Collette. "when giants still roamed the land, there lived a giant named Hector. He was over fifteen feet tall, too short to be a powerful giant, and yet too tall to fit in with the villagers. It was a sunny day, on the eve of his birthday, when Hector left his parent's house and began to walk away from the village . . ."

Did he run away?" cried Stevie. "Hey, Collette, did Hector run away?"

"Listen to the story, Stevie," suggested Collette.

"He's going to be in trouuu-ble!" cried Ginger Cillo.

"Let her finish!" snapped Kicky.

Collette nodded, then smiled at Kicky. "Thanks, Kicky. I know the kids are a little worried about Hector, but . . ."

"So finish the dumb story," ordered Kicky.

Collette glanced over at Marsha and Roger. Roger shrugged and Marsha rolled her eyes and looked up at the sky.

"Okay, sure," agreed Collette. She picked up the book and continued reading.

Collette was on the last page when she saw the first parent walking up the driveway. She glanced quickly at her watch. Holy cow, it was almost twelve o'clock! Collette saw Marsha, arms crossed, and slightly mad-looking, sitting on the picnic table, but Roger was leaning against the fence, smiling and enjoying the story. Collette kept reading.

When Collette finished, everyone clapped. She grinned. Even Jeff was now sitting on the edge of the blanket.

"I'll read you another story tomorrow," Collette promised.

"Good!"

"Read this story again!" insisted Wilbur. "I like Hector."

Hector the Giant had been a hit! Collette felt a rush of pride until she noticed Kicky, half hidden in the shade of the biggest tree, crying.

Chapter Nine

Monday, July 10th

Dear Sarah,

The first day of camp is finally over. It is only eight-thirty but I can barely keep my eyes open. We had a lot of fun but it is hard work!!!! Maybe you're working just as hard trying to have fun with ten thousand relatives.

I read a story today to the kids. It was about this giant named Hector who really isn't a human, but not really a giant. An in-between kind of guy. Any-

way, the kids were laughing at parts and then quiet, but they liked it. The foster girl, Kicky, was crying at the end. At first I started to walk over, but then I didn't. It's sooooo weird, Sarah. She's only ten, real skinny and usually kind of mean-looking. But, boy is she pretty when she's smiling and talking to her brother Eddie. Too bad she doesn't like anyone else.

Oooops. I just remembered. Kicky does like my mom. She was sitting on the porch talking to my mom a few times. Then when I tried to be nice and said, "Kicky, thanks for keeping my mom company because she doesn't feel too hot in the heat." (Ha, little joke there!) Kicky just said, "You don't look a thing like your mom."

Now what does that mean? Of course I don't. I have blonde hair and I am not nine months pregnant. But Kicky made it sound like I wasn't as NICE as my mom.

Oh, well, I'm tired. I wish you could be

here to meet this Kicky girl, Sarah. I
really can't figure her out.

Good-bye, I am falling asleep. I hope you
are having fun. Did you get your reunion
picture taken yet?

Love and Yawns,
Collette

Chapter Ten

Both Marsha and Roger came early the next morning. They were standing on Collette's back porch by eight-thirty.

"Collette," said Marsha breathlessly, leaning against the railing. "I was on your porch first, so *I* get to sign the clipboard first."

"What?" Collette went out on the porch.

"Marsha," began Roger. "You could have *slept* on Collette's porch last night and it wouldn't change the fact that my water balloon toss is going to be first. We didn't have time for it yesterday, so that's what we *start* with today."

"But, Roger, my little contest speech will take five minutes," pleaded Marsha. "Maybe only four minutes. And, anyway, kids don't want to get wet at nine o'clock in the morning."

"I do!" Stevie cried from the kitchen.

Laura, Jeff, and Stevie started laughing. The three of them were eating cold cereal and toast. Mr. Murphy had had to leave at seven and Collette had been put in charge.

"See?" said Roger. "Now, I'm going to go check out my balloons. Don't you dare mess with that schedule, Marsha."

"Okay, I have to finish eating and I'll be right out," said Collette.

Marsha followed Collette into the kitchen and sat down at the kitchen table. She picked up a piece of toast and added more jelly. "Boy, that Roger sure gets in the way."

"Hey, Marsha," said Stevie. "You're eating my mom's toast. We saved her that piece since it got a little burned up in the toaster."

Marsha took a small bite and looked around the kitchen. "Where *is* your mom?"

Laura set her spoon down and shook her head. "She's still asleep. Daddy told Collette she had to get us breakfast and make sure we were quiet."

"And to make sure Jeff stays a wimp," laughed

Stevie, ducking as Jeff reached over to give him a shove.

"I am way stronger than you, Stevie," insisted Jeff. "We bought you at a yard sale!"

Stevie laughed harder than ever.

"Hurry up, guys," said Collette. She drank the last of her juice and opened the dishwasher. "Rinse your dishes and put them in here. Jeff, you clear the table. Laura, go brush your hair, and Stevie, wipe off your face. It has jelly all over it."

Stevie gritted his teeth and held up both hands like a monster. "I is Hector, the jelly monster."

"You is Stevie, the wimp," laughed Jeff.

Marsha shook her head. "Your family is so weird, Collette. I can hardly wait to see what the baby's going to be like."

Collette peered out the kitchen window. "Marsha, we better get out there. The Cillo girls are walking up the driveway."

"Wait!" Marsha was behind Collette. "If Roger is going to go ahead with his water balloon idea, I think we should let the foster kids win. In fact, I have a special first prize for each of them."

"Marsha, that's nice. I thought you were tired

of trying with Kicky," reminded Collette. "You said she gave you a splitting headache."

Marsha rolled her eyes. "I was tired when I said that. And anyway, I felt terrible last night when I was sitting on the couch with my mom and dad, eating popcorn, feeling great as I told them all about camp." Marsha drew in a deep breath. "I want to make Kicky feel happy, not more miserable."

"I know." Collette smiled at Marsha. Even though Marsha lost her temper a lot, she was still one of the nicest girls Collette knew.

"So, when Roger is in the middle of his water balloon toss, I'll tell you my plan."

Collette's eyebrows went up. "Will I like it?"

"Trust me," laughed Marsha as she pushed past Collette and raced outside.

Within ten minutes, all the campers had arrived and Roger was lining up two teams for the water balloon toss. Collette was glad to see Kicky standing opposite Eddie, and Jeff opposite Stevie.

"Partners, get ready!" called out Roger. "On your mark, get set, *toss*!"

By the second toss, the Cillo girls were out and

Wilbur Platt was soaking wet. By the fourth toss, the left side of the line had backed up to the fence and only three kids on each side were left.

"I'm going to win!" shouted Stevie. "Come on, Jeff. Throw me some steam, baby!"

"No, sir. *We're* going to win, Stevie," laughed Eddie. "Kicky used to play on a real baseball team that had uniforms and everything."

Collette nudged Marsha. "Do you think that's true, Marsha? Sometimes I think Kicky makes up stuff to entertain Eddie."

Marsha shrugged. "Who knows? But I think this is when I better put my plan in motion."

Collette grabbed onto Marsha's arm. "What plan?"

Marsha held up two balloons. "The plan to make Kicky a winner. Look, I filled two balloons, but this one has a little less water in it so it's stronger. That's the one I'm going to give to Kicky and Eddie."

"But wait a minute, Marsha!" Collette grabbed her by the arm. "Isn't that cheating?"

"No," Marsha shot back. "It's called being nice to the foster kids, Collette. Isn't that what you told me to do?"

"Yes, I mean my mom wants us to be extra nice, but . . ."

Marsha blew her bangs up in the air. "So . . . so that is exactly what I'm trying to do."

"I know, but we don't have to rig up a contest, and . . ."

Marsha groaned. "Oh, for pete's sake, Collette. Make up your mind."

Marsha was trying to be nice to Kicky. And that was the most important thing, wasn't it?

"It sounds like a great idea," Collette said at last. "Go ahead."

Collette watched as Marsha hurried over and handed Kicky and Jeff each a red balloon. She felt like a traitor, watching how happy Stevie was to get a fresh balloon. He had no idea his big sister had just okayed his losing the match.

"Good luck, guys!" called out Marsha as she raced off the driveway. "May the best team win."

On the first toss with only three teams, an orange water balloon bounced once and splattered before Mikey Lister could ever catch it. That left just two teams: Jeff and Stevie, and Kicky and Eddie.

The first toss with just the two teams was perfect. The second toss was a little more dramatic. Collette gripped Marsha's arm as Stevie's balloon bounced once. Jeff swooped down and caught it, holding it high in the air.

"Oh, brother," muttered Marsha. "Jeff is too athletic."

During the third toss, Eddie caught his, then dropped it. Instead of breaking, the balloon bounced three times and stopped.

On the fourth toss, Jeff's balloon slid out of Stevie's hands and broke, splashing water all over his cowboy boots.

"Winners!" shouted Kicky, running over and hugging Eddie. "Way to go, Eddie."

"Thank goodness," sighed Collette. She glanced at her watch. They really better get going or they would be off schedule.

"First prize winners, congratulations!" shouted Marsha. She ran over to them both and, digging deep into her pockets, handed them each five dollars!

"Five dollars?" Collette bit her lip. "Holy cow!" Collette exchanged worried glances across the driveway with Roger. They had never discussed giving out money to the campers. It didn't sound

104

right. Marsha was sweet to try and give Kicky so much money, but maybe it was *too much.*

"Thanks," said Kicky, taking Eddie's and putting the money in her back pocket. "What a good prize!"

"Hey, all I got for a prize yesterday was a stuffed animal," wailed Matt. "That's not fair."

"Oh, phooey, Matt," said Marsha with a grin. "You like toys better than money, anyway. Come on guys, let's go sit under the tree and I'll tell you all about my contest."

"Can I win some more money?" laughed Eddie.

"Sure," agreed Marsha. "If you win first prize."

"Hey, Kicky!" Laura called. "Here's another prize."

Laura raced over and handed Kicky a bracelet. "You can keep it and everything."

Kicky smiled down at Laura. "Thanks. Is this for winning the water balloon toss?"

Laura grinned. "No. It's just 'cause you have to be a forester kid!"

Collette sighed, but Kicky's smile stayed on her face.

"Thanks, Laura," Kicky said. She slid the bracelet on her wrist. "Looks great."

"You look pretty wearing it," added Laura.

Collette let out a sigh of relief. Kicky seemed happy about the bracelet.

Collette watched as Marsha led the group over to the table. Kicky and Eddie raced to the lead. Kicky was actually smiling.

Roger dumped a handful of broken balloons into the trash can beside Collette. "I hope that *Big Spender Marsha* was using her own ten bucks for those prizes," Roger said. "Wasn't first prize supposed to be that rubber spider I brought in yesterday?"

Collette nodded. "Yeah, but I guess Marsha wanted the foster kids to have some money."

Roger shrugged. "Kids don't want money. I bet Eddie would have liked my spider."

Collette nodded, not quite sure what foster kids liked or needed most. Maybe money made them feel secure. She followed Roger back to the driveway, picking up soggy balloons.

As Collette looked up, she stopped. Maybe Marsha knew what she was doing after all. Kicky was finally laughing. In fact, she was helping Marsha organize the kids into a circle so they could all hear about the great contest.

"I guess Marsha knows what she's doing," Collette said at last.

Roger looked up and grinned at Collette. "Since when?"

"Shhhhhh. I want to hear what her contest is all about," said Collette.

"Okay, are you listening?" Marsha stood on top of the picnic bench. "Tomorrow, when you come to camp, we are going to have a happy hat contest!"

Lots of the little kids started to clap.

Roger poked Collette with his elbow. "So, did you know about this contest or did Marsha surprise you with it? Just like she surprised both of us by handing out ten bucks."

Collette shook her head. Marsha really should have mentioned it this morning. After all, they were all supposed to be in charge. But at least Marsha had been able to do what Collette or Roger hadn't been able to: make Kicky smile.

"Now, let me explain how this contest will work," continued Marsha. She held up a Pirates baseball cap. "When you go home tonight, I want you to ask your mom or dad for an old hat."

"Can it be a *new* hat?" asked Karen.

"Sure," agreed Marsha. "Old or new."

"Can it be a blue hat?" asked Mikey.

"Sure," Marsha said quickly.

Stevie waved his hand in the air. "Just not a dirty hat, right, Marsha? Just not a hat that fell in the mud."

"Right, now listen, guys. Once you get this hat," continued Marsha, "I want you to decorate it as fancy as you want. We are going to have a parade and the person with the greatest-looking hat will win a super-duper prize."

"I don't got no hats!" wailed Ginger Cillo.

"My dad has lots of hats!" shouted Wilbur. "His hair fell out and no more grew on his head. So then my mommy tolded him to wear a hat, and then my dad said — "

"Okay, thanks, Wilbur," broke in Marsha. "Now if you can't find a hat, just make one out of paper."

"We don't got no paper!" Ginger shouted out again. "Mommy gives all the paper back to the stores."

Marsha paused for a second, tapping her whistle against her hand. "Well, listen, Ginger. If you don't have any hats or paper, or glue, or paste or anything else . . . just come down to my house after camp and I'll loan you some."

A few kids clapped. Collette was glad to see Kicky smiling at Marsha.

"Will you give me a hat, too?" asked Eddie. "I left my hats at my real house."

Marsha nodded. "Sure, Eddie. Anyone who needs a hat, just come to my house today. Okay? Now let's all sit back and let me talk, okay? Now, after you get your hat, and decorate it, I want you to wear it to camp tomorrow. Use lots of decorations."

Stevie stood up and walked toward Marsha. "Hey, wait a second, Marsha. My mommy putted all of our decorations in the attic. Even our angel and our star."

Marsha groaned. "No, Stevie. Not your Christmas decorations. I want you guys to use stuff from around the house. Like glitter, or buttons, or maybe some pretty feathers. I want to see who can make their hat the prettiest."

A few kids clapped again.

"Marsha has a cool idea," admitted Roger. "I'll bring a cassette player. The kids could parade to the music, like in a pageant."

"Great." Collette would be sure and remind Marsha that it had been Roger's idea to bring the music. They were really starting to work as a team!

"Is first prize more money?" asked Eddie.

Marsha laughed. "Something even better than money!"

More kids laughed and clapped.

"The girl really knows how to work a crowd," whispered Roger. Collette wasn't positive, but she thought Roger looked kind of proud.

Marsha blasted her whistle to quiet the kids. "First prize will be a lot of fun for everyone . . . especially me."

"What is it?" called out Jeff.

Marsha held up both hands and waited for the kids to get quiet. Then she smiled sweetly right over at Collette and Roger.

Collette smiled back. Wait till she wrote Sarah about how wonderful everything was finally turning out!

"First prize for the best happy hat, will be a chance to drop a bag of ice down Roger Friday's back."

All of the kids started to hoot and yell, laughing hard.

"What?" Roger cried.

"That will make Roger do the happy hat hop!" laughed Marsha.

Roger opened his mouth and shouted something back, but Collette couldn't hear above the laughter. The only thing she caught was the anger in Roger's eyes.

Chapter Eleven

"I'm quitting," announced Roger.

"No, you're not," said Collette. She grabbed Roger by the arm. "Please!"

"Unless you do something about Marsha, I'm quitting," said Roger. "And this time I mean it."

"I'll talk to her," promised Collette. "Don't quit, Roger. I need you here."

"Yeah, and I need Marsha making me look like a fool like I need a hole in the head," muttered Roger. "I only agreed to do this because John said it would be fun."

"I'll talk to Marsha," repeated Collette. Her head was beginning to pound. She didn't even want to think of the next three hours. With Roger mad at

Marsha, the day was going to go slower than ever.

Marsha and Roger were cool to each other for the rest of the morning. Mrs. Murphy came out and taught everyone how to make s'mores on the grill. Then Roger's mom arrived and set up a bowling alley in the driveway. That was so much fun the next two activities had to be canceled so everyone could play an extra game.

"Thank goodness for mothers!" announced Collette as Mrs. Friday loaded the bowling equipment back in her car. Right after she said it, she felt bad, hoping Kicky and Eddie didn't feel left out. But when Collette looked over, Kicky was busy at the craft table with Mrs. Murphy.

As soon as the last camper was picked up, Collette ordered Marsha and Roger to sit down under the shade tree and talk to each other.

"Now this war between you two has got to stop," Collette said. "I can see why our teachers went nuts with you two fighting so much." Collette drew in a deep breath and tried to talk calmly. "We're *supposed* to be a team," insisted Collette. "You two can't be mad at each other."

"Watch me," Roger said shortly.

"It was a *joke*, Roger," insisted Marsha. She

took off her whistle and spun it around her wrist. "I mean, I didn't say that first prize was the chance to pour hot *tar* down your back."

Roger made a face at Marsha. "Only because you didn't think of it fast enough."

"I can out-think you any day of the week, Friday," Marsha shot back.

Collette blasted her whistle. "Hey, come on, guys, stop fighting. Start acting like a team. Now, you two declare a truce so we can finish cleaning up and plan some neat stuff for tomorrow."

"Yeah, like a new first prize for Marsha's little contest," suggested Roger. "You're just jealous because those kids think I'm cooler than you. But I'm a counselor here, too, and I don't want a bunch of little kids laughing at me like I'm some clown."

"You *are* a clown, Friday. Besides, a few ice cubes won't hurt you." Marsha stood up and started to stack the paints back in her craft box. "They might even shrink that swelled head of yours! Just let a kid drop one cube, one measly cube down your back."

"No," Roger said.

Collette's head jerked up. She didn't like the

way Roger's "no" came out. It was short and hard, like striking a match.

Marsha just laughed. "Roger, it will be funny."

"No way."

Collette glanced up at Roger. She felt like she was watching the beginnings of a very dangerous tennis match.

Marsha sighed. "I already announced it and the kids went wild. They loved the idea. Now, we *can't* disappoint the little kids, can we?"

"I'm not changing my mind," said Roger. "I guess you'll just have to admit you made a mistake."

Marsha tugged at her bangs. "Okay, I made a mistake. I was just trying to be funny or something. But I can't just change the first prize, can I? Roger, did you see Kicky laughing today? I mean, we are finally making some sort of progress with that kid, and if I have to get up and start taking back promises, she will end up not trusting us. Is that what you want?"

Roger got up from the back step and held out both hands. "Hey, all I want is to be *no* part of your stupid contest, Marsha. But if your first prize happy hat winner takes one step toward me with an ice cube in his hand, I'm walking."

Marsha groaned. "You are *so* dramatic, Roger. Honestly."

Collette followed Roger down the driveway. "We'll change it tomorrow, Roger, okay? Don't even *think* about quitting. The little campers really like you."

"Well, they like *me*, too," said Marsha. She hurried to catch up. "I mean, I don't think it's fair that you are taking Roger's side in this, Collette. I have been busy thinking up most of the fun activities in this camp, in case you haven't noticed. I did almost all of the planning for this camp."

Collette stopped and turned back to face Marsha. "We have all thought of fun activities, Marsha, and I am not taking *anyone's* side, either. I just think it's kind of dumb for us to start fighting with each other."

Collette stopped and drew in a deep breath. She could tell that Marsha was getting mad now, too. "All we have to do is change the first prize for your happy hat contest. What's the big deal?"

"Yeah, what's the big deal?" Roger wanted to know.

Marsha swung her whistle faster and faster around her wrist. Collette watched, afraid if Marsha got any madder she might just take off like a helicopter and disappear from Pittsburgh completely.

"The big deal *is* . . ." began Marsha slowly, marching her words out one by one, "is that I am tired of you and Mr. Roger Friday telling me what to do, okay? No one is the boss of me. I have tried real hard to make Kicky laugh and I finally got her to start smiling and I don't think one crummy little ice cube is going to hurt him, okay? The only reason he doesn't want to do it is because I thought of it." Marsha took a step closer. "My idea for the hat contest was terrific, Roger. I know what kids like. Kicky has been in a good mood ever since I had the great idea of giving her five bucks. You heard those campers laughing and you can't stand the thought of anyone being funnier than you."

Roger stuck his face next to Marsha's. "Hey you're no competition, Marsha, cause you're not *funny . . . you're just plain nuts.*"

Marsha's mouth fell open, then clamped down hard. She looked over at her house. "I don't have

117

to stand here and listen to this junk. I don't even *need* to work for my summer money. My dad pays me ten dollars a week, just . . . just to be me."

"Yeah, well the guy is being short-changed then."

Collette pushed in between them. "Stop it!"

The three of them stood in a circle, each glaring at the other.

"I refuse to take orders from Roger," grumbled Marsha.

Roger frowned back. "And I don't take orders from you, either."

"Guys, we're supposed to be a *team*," reminded Collette quietly. Her head was beginning to pound. If only Sarah were here to help dilute Marsha and Roger's war. She wished she could get out the garden hose and squirt them both down her driveway. It was one thing to listen to little campers fight over who got to use the red dump truck in the sandbox first, but it really sounded awful to listen to the counselors arguing.

Roger took a step back and handed Collette a whistle. "Hey, I don't care who's in charge. But I don't take orders from Marsha Cessano. I only did this to help you out."

"Roger!" Collette tried to hand him back his whistle.

"And we only asked you because *John* wanted you," snapped Marsha.

"Be quiet, Marsha," shouted Collette. Roger's face flashed mad-red, and then settled into hurt in less than a second.

Roger turned and walked toward his bike. Collette yanked down hard on Marsha's arm. "You tell Roger you're sorry right now or I'll never work at a summer camp with you again."

Marsha covered her eyes with both hands. "You are so bossy, Collette. Just wait till I write Sarah tonight."

Collette took another step closer to Marsha. "I mean it, Marsha. We have been planning this camp for weeks. Now apologize!"

Marsha shook off Collette's arm and crossed her own. "Oh, okay. Roger, I-am-sorry. There."

Roger walked his bike back and stopped in front of Collette and Marsha. He tapped his fingers against his silver handlebars for a long time. Then he reached out and took the whistle back from Collette. "See you tomorrow," he said quietly.

Chapter Twelve

Tuesday, July 11

Dear Sarah,

Today was the second day of camp. Right now, I think you are lucky to be in Ohio. (Just kidding . . . or maybe I'm not.) If you got a letter from Marsha, please remember that she is only telling her side. I know I am only telling my side, but let's face it, Sarah, I think I stay a little calmer than Marsha. Roger and Marsha have already had one big fight, but Marsha and I have already had one little fight. *Marsha always thinks I am trying to be in charge. I'm not. I just want everyone to get along. Besides, I think I do know a little bit more about kids than she does, Sarah. I don't mean to brag, but I am a big sister to three kids and Marsha doesn't even have a dog. Kicky is finally acting like she likes camp. And Marsha is really good with her. Kicky sure is a good older sister. Eddie got stung by a bee today and Kicky got my mom and had ice on his hand before I even knew what happened. Kicky really likes my mom. Kicky carried the milk box up on the back porch so my mom could put her feet up.*

John is okay. He may stop by on Thursday. His mom said he can still play in the tennis tournament.

> *Love,*
> *Your tired Best Friend,*
> *Collette*

Chapter Thirteen

At nine o'clock the next morning, Collette slapped Marsha and Roger a high five. "Congratulations, team! You two have been together ten minutes and not one fight. Plus, all fifteen campers came back for the third day. We must be doing a good job."

"Kicky is wearing the bracelet Laura gave her and actually came up and asked if I needed any help," said Marsha.

"Did you tell her you were looking for a good psychiatrist?" asked Roger.

Collette cringed, waiting for Marsha to explode.

"Yeah," laughed Marsha. "I told her I get a discount since I sold your brain to their lab."

Roger grinned. "Pretty smooth, Cessano."

Marsha made a small bow. "Anyway," continued Marsha, "I knew all the campers would come back. Everyone looks great in their hats. Boy, oh boy, when I have a good idea, I really have a *good* idea."

"Don't break your arm trying to pat yourself on the back, Marsha." Roger reached down and picked up two yellow buckets. Each bucket contained plastic baggies filled with jelly beans. "Just wait until you see the kids with the bean bag toss. Yo, kids! Jelly bean bag time! Winners get to eat the jelly beans."

"I want five bucks," laughed Eddie.

Marsha bit her lip. "Gosh, maybe I should run home and get some money in case one of the foster kids wins."

"Jelly beans are fine," said Roger. "Who wants to play?"

Collette laughed as the campers started to cheer.

"But . . . but, wait a minute," cried Marsha. She grabbed Roger by the back of his shirt. "Roger, can't we start with the happy hat contest? The kids are already wearing their hats and your jelly bean bag toss will mess them up. Please, let me go first, Roger."

Roger tapped his finger on Collette's clipboard. "No way. You've got to learn to work as a team, Marsha. I don't see your hat contest marked down under nine o'clock activities. And I *do see* my jelly bean bag toss. We told you yesterday that you have to write down your time slot so we won't get confused." Roger wiggled his eyebrows up and down. "The bottom line is, I'm *in* and you're *out*."

Marsha grabbed the clipboard from Collette. "What . . . what are you talking about? Let me see. Where?" Marsha scowled as Collette pointed out Roger's printing. "You got here earlier than I did this morning. That's no fair. Besides, who said we had to start writing down our times and activities? When Sarah was part of this camp, she never voted that we had to write down time slots. Whose bright idea was this?"

Roger picked up his buckets. "Collette and I had a little meeting before you arrived and we *both* thought it would be a good idea. This way we won't be fighting."

"What? What?" Marsha sputtered. "You guys

had a meeting without me? Without the *main* counselor?"

Collette held out the clipboard toward Marsha. "Well, it wasn't really a . . . a meeting, Marsha. It was more of a talk. You see, I thought it might help to keep us organized if we always wrote down our ideas for activities, and then followed the list. That way we could each pick at least two activities to do with the kids and . . ."

Marsha crossed her arms and shot Roger another mean look. "And of course you let Roger pick the first activity. He got first crack at the little *meeting* you both forgot to invite me to. Thanks a lot, Collette."

Collette gripped the clipboard a little more tightly. Marsha was trying her hardest to make a big deal out of this, to make a big deal out of everything! "It wasn't a . . . a *meeting*. I didn't plan this ahead of time. Roger just walked up the driveway first, and I told him my idea of listing the activities and he agreed. Then he jotted down his jelly bean bag toss. You can have the second activity, Marsha. I'm willing to go third."

"Oh, *thanks a lot*, Collette, for such a great

honor. I mean, since this is your backyard you think you are the head counselor or something. All you do is walk around with your clipboard and make sure Roger and I are doing all the work."

"No, I don't." Collette looked at the yard. Most of the kids were lining up for the jelly bean bag toss, but a few were wandering around the yard while others were playing in the sandbox. "I'm not the only one in charge, Marsha. We all are. But, let's go over and help Roger with his jelly bean bag toss."

Kicky walked up and pulled on Collette's arm. "Hey, you two better get back to work. Kids are throwing sand. Eddie got some in his eye already."

Collette took a few steps toward the sandbox. "Jeff, tell the kids to stop throwing sand."

Collette smiled at Kicky. "Thanks, Kicky. We're going to start taking roll in just a few minutes. My mom is setting up the craft table if you want to go look it over."

Kicky nodded. "Your mom doesn't look too hot this morning, Collette. Why don't you tell her to sit and rest on the porch? She can watch us from there. I can help you with the crafts if you need help."

"Okay, thanks." Collette turned to Marsha. "Maybe you could go over and help Roger while I take roll and get the next activity set up."

"No, thanks."

"Come on, Marsha," pleaded Collette.

"No," said Marsha quietly. She sighed and sat on the bottom step. "I'd like to help you and Roger, but I'm afraid I'm on *break* right now."

"What?" Collette spun around. "What break?"

Marsha grinned. "Oh, gosh. Don't tell me I forgot to write down, *Marsha on Break!*" Marsha sighed. "I guess since I missed the morning meeting, I didn't know I was *supposed* to mark it on the clipboard."

"You're unreal, Marsha. Camp just started. It's nine-oh-three. You haven't done anything to take a break *from*," Collette sputtered. "Besides, we've never talked about breaks. Go help Roger with his jelly bean bag toss."

Marsha pretended to yawn. She stretched both arms high over her head. "We never talked about this *clipboard idea*, either, Collette. I'm in just as much charge as you are and *I* say that I get a fifteen minute break every morning before nine-thirty."

"What? That's dumb, Marsha." Collette reached down and tried to pull Marsha up off the step. "This isn't funny. You have to help or you can't be part of the camp."

Marsha shook back her hair and got up off the stairs. "Oh, boy, you sure sound like you're the boss of the camp, Collette. Wait till I tell Sarah about how bossy you're acting. She will be sooooo glad she went to Ohio."

"I sure wish she *had* stayed home, Marsha," snapped Collette. "And, I am not bossy. You're the one acting like some . . . some dictator person. You can't go on break now with all these little kids waiting for us. We're supposed to be a team. Now just come on and help and we can talk about it later, okay?"

Without waiting for an answer, Collette turned and hurried over to Roger. As soon as camp was over today, she was going to have to force Roger and Marsha to sit down together, *again*, so they could all talk about the rules. Not the rules for the little kids; the rules for the counselors.

Collette could see that Roger's jelly bean bag toss was off to a slow start. While Roger was busy explaining the rules, some of the little kids were sitting down, eating the jelly beans, and others were throwing them up in the air and catching them all by themselves. Matt was busy trying to trade his black jelly beans for red ones.

"Hey . . . stop that, guys!" shouted Roger. "If you eat all your jelly beans, you won't have anything to toss. Matt, hey, leave Karen's red jelly beans alone." Roger gave two sharp blasts from his whistle. "Now, this game is just like the water balloon toss that we had yesterday. Remember how much fun that was? Okay, now, I want everyone to hold on to your bags till I finish explaining about the game." Roger clapped his hands but none of the little kids seemed to stop doing what they were doing. "Now . . . now listen, guys. Pick a partner. You are going to throw your jelly bean bag to this person."

"Roger, Roger, wait a minute. I don't like black jelly beans!" complained Matt. "They make me throw up."

"No, sir!" cried his brother, Mikey. "Pizza makes you throw up."

"Black jelly beans, too," insisted Matt. " 'Member when I throwed up in my Easter basket and . . ."

Roger blasted his whistle again. "Stop talking about throwing up. We're here to have fun, right guys? Remember now. I don't want you to start tossing until I blow my whistle. Understand? Now, when you hear my whistle you can start. Okay? Ready, guys?"

"Oh, *grooooosssssssssss!*" screamed Marsha. She raced into the middle of the driveway and threw a bag of jelly beans on the ground. "Nobody touch your jelly beans."

Marsha grabbed Eddie's bag of jelly beans, peered inside, and tossed them on the ground, too. "Oh, cripes! There are millions of spider eggs on those jelly beans!"

"What? Spiders!!!" Karen and Ginger threw their jelly beans into the air and started to scream. Matt and Mikey started to laugh and began chasing the other campers around the driveway, waving their jelly bean bags in the air. Pretty soon all the campers were throwing their jelly bean bags around. No one was trying to catch any.

"Stand back! Here comes the spider-man smasher!" Stevie snapped his goggles over his eyes and started smashing jelly beans as fast as he could.

"Disgusting!" screamed Laura as she zoomed into the garage.

Roger threw down his hat and started blowing his whistle blast after blast till his face was as red as his shirt.

"Stop it . . . wait . . . there are no spiders!" he shouted.

Collette ran from kid to kid, telling them it was just a joke. "Hey, calm down, guys. Marsha was kidding. Don't cry, Ginger. Stop crying, Karen." Collette picked up Karen and gave her a hug. "Don't cry. This is supposed to be fun."

It took over five minutes to calm everyone down. And even then, the only one who was left smiling was Marsha. Marsha stood on the back porch, wearing a silly grin and tapping her shiny silver whistle on Collette's clipboard.

"Marsha!" snapped Collette. "Are you nuts? Why did you tell them there were spiders on their jelly beans? You ruined everything."

Marsha just shrugged and pointed to the clipboard. "Sorry, I was only trying to speed things along. Now that the toss is over, we're ready for the happy hat contest."

Collette glared at Marsha.

"Okay, Marsha," growled Roger as he charged across the driveway. He took the back stairs, two at a time, and stood nose to nose with Marsha. "Did you flick your brain to *off*, or did it finally turn to dust?"

"Ha, ha," said Marsha. "Very funny."

"Yeah," muttered Roger. "You're about as funny as a forest fire."

"Your opinion," huffed Marsha back. But she said it quietly. And she was tugging on her bangs like she was starting to get nervous.

Collette sighed. Why couldn't the Marsha-Roger war be over? If it kept up any longer, Camp Summer Fun would be over.

Collette looked over at Kicky, who had her arm around Eddie and was frowning at Marsha. Marsha was frowning at Roger, and judging from the look on Roger's face, Camp Summer Fun had just been tossed into a major civil war.

Chapter Fourteen

While Mrs. Murphy organized a "follow-the-leader" game, Collette ordered Roger and Marsha back under the tree for a quick conference.

"Okay, okay, *okay*, Roger. I already said I was sorry," groaned Marsha. "It was a *joke*. How many times do I have to tell you? It was a joke!"

"Very *funny*, Marsha." Roger spat the words out like they were burning his tongue. "Excuse me if I forgot to laugh. I thought we agreed yesterday to end this stupid war."

Collette was glad to see Marsha look embarrassed. "How was I supposed to know the kids would spaz out like that? I thought it would be . . . well, funny."

Roger dropped two handfuls of jelly beans into the trash. "You could have turned on your brain, Marsha. I guess you know now the kids didn't think it was too funny. Kicky took Eddie over by the wall."

Marsha brushed past Roger. "Okay, okay, I get the message. We better get back to work." She turned back and looked worried. "Roger, you aren't going to try to ruin *my* activity, are you?"

Collette groaned. If Roger tried to get even, she would have to cancel camp. The campers didn't sign up for a week of "let's-see-who-can-get-even-last"!

Roger just shook his head. "Don't worry, Marsha. I think one *jerk* per camp is enough."

Marsha's face flushed red, but she didn't say anything back. She looked more sad than mad, almost like she was beginning to agree with Roger.

"Well, good then," Marsha finally said. "As soon as the kids finish follow-the-leader, I'll get my parade going so I can pick a winner for the happy — "

"Collette," interrupted Roger. "I'm going to get the markers for the mural. Your mom said we could nail it right to the garage door." Roger started to walk away, then turned back. "And by the way, Marsha. If you try to sabotage this activity, I'm coming after you."

Collette's head jerked up. It was beginning to sound like a bad western movie. Any minute now Roger would lasso Marsha and tie her to the fence. Collette stole a look at Marsha, hoping she wasn't going to throw an insult back. But Marsha's head was down.

Roger slammed the door. Collette and Marsha both stared at the ground. Collette didn't know if she should try to convince Marsha that she wasn't a jerk, or yell at Marsha for *being* a jerk.

"Hey, girls, our game is over. Time to get back to work," called Mrs. Murphy. "The natives are getting restless, and I'm going to go inside for ten minutes to lie down. Come and get me if you need help."

Collette noticed that Kicky smiled at Mrs. Murphy. Kicky had been trailing Mrs. Murphy like a shadow all morning.

"Okay, Mom," Collette called back. She picked up her clipboard. She was glad her mom was going inside. She really did look extra tired today.

135

"Your mom's right. I better get the happy hat contest going," Marsha said finally. She gave a loud blast with her whistle and marched into the center of the yard. "Okay, kids. Line up for the happy hat contest."

It was great to hear everyone laughing and clapping.

"I couldn't find a hat!" whined Tracy. "My mom said I have to borrow one from you guys."

Collette turned and pulled a straw hat from the dress-up basket. "Here, Tracy. Go get in line."

"Thanks!" Tracy raced across the lawn, waving her hat around and around in the air.

"Line up kids!" shouted Marsha. She climbed on top of the picnic table and gave three sharp toots. "Come on, guys. Let me see how fancy you look."

Roger pushed open the screen door with his foot, balancing a tray filled with markers, paints, and brushes, with a roll of mural paper stuck under his arm. "Is she finished yet?"

Collette giggled. "She just started. But the kids seem excited." Collette took the roll of paper from Roger and led the way down the steps. "I'll help you set up."

"Now, I want everyone to put on their hats and then get in line," called out Marsha. "We're going to have a parade so I can choose the winner."

"Hey, stop pushing, Matt," complained Ginger. "Marsha, tell Matt to stop licking my hat."

"Listen up, you guys," ordered Marsha. "Put your hat on and then get in line. Hey, Mikey . . . I don't think Karen wants you to try on her hat."

Collette turned around and grinned at Roger. Marsha was having a little trouble getting her troops assembled. Part of Collette wanted to run over and help. But it was kind of nice to see Marsha *needing* help.

Roger laughed. "Looks like there is a little bit of trouble in paradise over there. Let's check the clipboard and see if we're signed up to help her."

Collette laughed. If the kids got any noisier, she would have to go over. After all, they were a team.

"Eddie, you and Kicky get in line," Marsha called out. "Come on, now. I need everyone in line before I can start the parade."

"I don't *want* to get in line." Eddie walked slowly across the yard to Collette and Roger. He took off his hat and tossed it on the grass. "I don't want to be in the parade. My hat is dumb."

"No, it's not," Collette said quickly.

"Yes, it is," said Eddie. "Kicky said."

Collette glanced down at the worn cowboy hat. It had no decoration. "Your hat looks nice, Eddie. I like cowboy hats."

Eddie shook his head. "It's not so good. Kicky said we shouldn't look dumb 'cause people will make fun of us."

"Was Mrs. Lister too busy to help you with your hat?" asked Collette.

"No, she wanted to. She found me this old hat in the toy box. Then she said she could help me glue stars on it, but Kicky said that we didn't need her help." Eddie looked up and his eyes started to fill. "Kicky doesn't want Mrs. Lister to get too tired of us. But maybe we could have used a little help." Collette looked up and spotted the Lister boys. Matt was wearing a snow cap with buttons glued on and Mikey was wearing a straw hat with *Greetings from New Mexico* stitched in red and a green balloon tied on top.

"Mrs. Lister likes helping, Eddie," said Collette.

Eddie nodded. "Yeah, I know. She's a *real* nice lady. She said Kicky could wear her feather hat," explained Eddie. "But Kicky was afraid she might

138

get it dirty. Kicky said we shouldn't make extra work for Mrs. Lister since her kids are so crazy. If a foster mom gets worn out, that's when they send you back." Eddie sighed and nudged his hat with his tennis shoe. "Then you have to go to a *new* foster home."

Roger's face went pale beneath his tan. He shot Collette a worried look before he put his hand on Eddie's shoulder. "Hey, Eddie," said Roger. He knelt down beside Eddie and picked up his hat. "You know what? This hat looks a lot like one I had when I was in the second grade. Mine was even more smashed. It looked like a truck ran over it. Man, was it cool. I loved it."

Eddie shook his head. "Kicky said one day we won't ever have to wear other people's old stuff, ever again."

Roger tapped Eddie on the knee. "Well, sometimes old stuff is real comfortable. Lots of people pay money to buy old stuff."

Eddie smiled. "Could I sell it?"

"Maybe!" laughed Roger. "When you grow up and get famous, then everyone will want this old hat."

Collette frowned at Roger. She knew he was

only trying to cheer Eddie up, but making up stories wasn't going to make him stay happy for long.

"Now you get back in line and in a few minutes you can come over here and I'll teach you how to draw a real cowboy, wearing the hat you have in your hand."

"Cool!" cried Eddie, pulling the hat down low over his eyes. "How do I look?"

"Great," Roger and Collette said together. Collette could see Kicky in the sandbox. She was still watching Eddie, but at least she wasn't standing two inches away. Maybe she was finally beginning to trust Collette and Roger with her little brother.

"Hey, Roger," said Eddie, pushing his hat up with his fist. "If my hat is worth lots of money one day, do you know what I'm going to do with the money?"

"What?"

Eddie swallowed hard. "Give it to my mom. Kicky said that our mom got sick cause we didn't have too much money. My mom worked too hard at her jobs."

Collette felt chills on her arms. Roger must have

realized he had carried his story too far, because his face tightened.

Collette put her arm around Eddie. "That's real nice, Eddie. I bet your mom misses you and Kicky a lot."

Eddie nodded. "Me, too."

"Hey, you know what, Eddie?" said Roger. "Collette and I have a box with glitter stars and glue and even green feathers over at the craft table. Let's go over and fix your hat up real fast? Before Marsha's contest starts."

"Then could I sell my hat for money?" Eddie looked hopeful.

"Not right away," Roger said slowly.

Disappointment washed over Eddie's face.

"Collette! Collette, look at me!"

Collette spun around. Stevie stood on the back porch, both hands outstretched as if he were about to do an amazing magic trick.

"Do you like my hat, Collette?"

"Looks great, Stevie," said Collette, barely glancing up at her little brother. She looked down at her clipboard. Nine activities to go.

Collette tapped her pencil against the clipboard and sighed.

Too bad she couldn't write down a way to make Eddie and Kicky happier on her activity sheet. Then her camp would really be a success.

"You better get in line, Stevie," Collette called out. "The parade is about to start."

"Wow! Look at Stevie's hat!" cried Eddie. "I bet he wins first prize in the contest. Cool!"

Collette nodded at Eddie. Stevie had been talking about his secret hat all morning. No one was allowed to see it until the contest started. Collette just hoped he hadn't glued cereal and feathers all over her mother's new gardening hat.

Roger whistled. "Uh-oh. You better check Stevie's hat out, Collette."

Something in Roger's voice caused Collette to look up. She took a few steps closer, then a few more. She gasped when she noticed the glistening pearls and gold chains set in thick globs of white school paste atop Stevie's Pirates cap. The hat sparkled in the early morning sun.

"Oh, my gosh," Collette whispered. "Oh, my gosh!" she cried more loudly as she stared at the center of Stevie's hat. Even from a distance, she recognized the dazzling gleam of Great-Aunt Helen's red ruby ring!

Chapter Fifteen

"Stevie!" Collette ran across the yard to the porch. "Stevie Murphy! What do you think you're doing with Mom's best jewelry?"

Stevie put both hands on his hat and took three steps backward until he bumped into the door. "Nothing. I need it for my hat." Stevie put both hands over his head. "Don't take it off, Collette. Mommy wasn't going to wear this stuff today! She just tolded me that her tummy hurts. She's taking a rest on the couch."

Collette tried to take the hat, but Stevie turned and buried his head in the screen door. "Don't touch it, Collette! Mommy won't care."

"Stevie, turn around and let me see what you

have on there. You can't use Aunt Helen's ring! Mom said she was going to give it to me when I turned sixteen. Come on, Stevie, turn around."

"No. Go away, Collette."

"What's all the yelling about?" asked Jeff from the other side of the screen door. "Mom doesn't feel well so stop yelling."

Stevie pressed his face up against the screen door. "Come out here and make Collette be nice to me, Jeff. She won't let me be in Marsha's contest! She doesn't like my great hat!"

"I like your hat," said Wilbur from the bottom of the steps.

"Me, too," announced Eddie. He turned around. "Hey, Kicky, don't you like Stevie's hat?"

"Looks good to me," said Kicky.

Collette groaned. Lots of little campers were coming closer to see what all the noise was about. "Stevie has to get a new hat. Then you can be in the contest, Stevie. You can't wear Mom's best jewelry. Now give me that hat!"

"No!" shouted Stevie.

"And let me outside, Stevie," ordered Jeff. "Hurry up, too, 'cause this tray is heavy."

"Give me the ring, Stevie!" ordered Collette. "And the pearls."

Stevie spun around, fat tears rolling down his smeared cheeks. "You guys is so mean. If you take off the good stuff, then my hat will look dumb."

"Get out of the way of this door, or you *will* be dumb," said Jeff. "Hurry up before I spill something."

"What's wrong, Stevie?" Kicky stood beside Collette. "Who's being mean to you?"

"No one," snapped Collette. She felt surrounded.

"What's the matter?" asked Marsha. "Everyone left my hat parade."

"Nothing," said Collette quickly. Then she turned and tried to smile at the campers. "Nothing is wrong, guys. Go back and line up for the parade."

"Something is too wrong," wailed Stevie.

"Stevie, hurry up and move!" shouted Jeff. "If I drop this stuff, it's going to be all your fault."

"Hey, what's wrong, Collette?" asked Roger. He hurried to the bottom of the stairs. "Why is everyone yelling?"

" 'Cause they is so mean!" sobbed Stevie. He wiped under each eye with the back of his arm. "My hat was good. Now you big guys won't let me be in Marsha's contest."

"Leave Stevie alone," called out Eddie.

"Eddie!" said Kicky. Her voice sounded angry. "Come on, Eddie. Let's go sit under the tree till this fighting is over."

"No one is *fighting*," said Collette quickly. She smiled at Kicky to let her know that everything was okay. She smiled at the campers. She was in charge. She couldn't let a family fight get in the way of running the camp. Once everyone went home, she could yell at Stevie.

"So why are you yelling at your brother?" asked Kicky. She reached out and pulled Eddie next to her. "You're supposed to take care of him. That's what big sisters are for, lady."

"Yeah. And anyway, he didn't do nothing!" said Eddie. "His hat looks nice. Let him get in Marsha's parade. He might win. He could give the prize to his mom."

"Yeah," mumbled Stevie. "Mommy would feel better then."

"Quit trying to be a cop and let your brother wear the hat!" snapped Kicky. "You sure make a big deal out of everything."

"It *is* a big deal!" Collette shot back.

Kicky's eyes opened wide, but Collette thought she saw a slight smile.

"It isn't funny!" added Collette.

Collette reached out and grabbed Stevie's hand. "Come with me, Stevie. I want to look at your hat."

Jeff pushed open the door and carried a huge plastic tray and a plastic bottle of apple juice down the stairs. "Boy, Stevie," said Jeff. "If Mom sees you with her good jewelry on, you're a dead man!"

"I don't want to be a dead man," wailed Stevie. He took off his happy hat and threw it on the ground. "I just wanted to win a prize. Now you guys is mad at me."

"Listen, Stevie," said Collette quickly. "Nobody is mad at you. But pick up the hat and put it on my bed. Then I'll put the rings and necklaces back in Mom's jewelry case, and she won't have to get upset."

Kicky reached out for the hat. "I'll put it inside."

"Boy," muttered Jeff as he walked by. "If Mom sees that hat, she's going to be so mad, steam will come out of her ears."

"For real?" asked Stevie. He shifted from one foot to the next. "Will fire come out?"

"No, but she'll be upset. Don't ever go in Mom's jewelry box again." said Collette. "Ever."

"Okay," said Stevie.

"And stay out of trouble for the rest of the day," added Collette.

"Okay."

"In fact, stay out of trouble for the rest of my camp week." Collette tapped her whistle against her hand. "I told Mom that brothers shouldn't come to my camp."

Stevie lowered his head.

"Okay," he answered quietly.

"Now, let's get back in line, kids!" announced Collette.

Just then, Roger flipped on Marsha's tape deck. Out blasted "Easter Parade." As if by magic, the kids started to follow Roger like the Pied Piper. Roger picked up the tape deck and walked around the huge shade tree. Then he handed the tape deck to Marsha. "Start the parade, Marsha."

Collette smiled. Marsha sure owed Roger one. He could have stood by and let her parade go to pieces, but he didn't.

"Hey, Kicky," called out Jeff. "Where are you going with Stevie's hat?"

Kicky turned, her hand on the screen door. "I was going to put it inside. So nothing would get lost."

"Well, my mom is resting on the couch, so be quiet," called out Jeff.

"I will," said Kicky. She actually smiled.

Collette handed Jeff the clipboard. "Go help Marsha with the parade. I'll fix Mom's jewelry. I want to clean the glue off the ring before she sees it."

"Okay," said Jeff.

Collette took the hat from Kicky on the porch and they both walked inside. "Want to help me clean off the ring and pearls?" Collette was starting to feel better now that she finally had the hat back.

"Sure," said Kicky.

"My brother has some crazy ideas," said Collette.

"He's funny," laughed Kicky.

"This hat wasn't funny." Collette scowled at Stevie's creation. As she turned it around in her hands, she froze.

Great-Aunt Helen's ruby ring was gone!

Chapter Sixteen

"Oh my gosh!" cried Collette. "Oh my gosh!"

"What's wrong?" asked Kicky. "You okay?"

"No! The ring!" cried Collette. "Aunt Helen's ring isn't on the hat anymore." Collette turned around and retraced her steps to the back door. "Where could it be?"

"I don't know."

"Well, did you see it drop? Was the ring on the hat when you had it?"

"I never had it, Collette."

"Yes, you did, Kicky. I took it from you."

"Well, *you* had it then," snapped Kicky. "Okay, I'll help you look. Is it worth a lot of money?"

"Yes. A whole lot." Collette's voice was shaky.

"Plus, my mom was going to . . . to give it to me when I turned sixteen."

"Well, I don't know where the ring is," said Kicky. "Let's look outside."

Collette pulled open the kitchen pantry door and placed the hat inside on top of the cereal boxes. She didn't want her mother to walk in and find the hat now.

Collette and Kicky hurried outside and down the stairs. Marsha's little holiday hatters were still marching around the shade tree.

"We were standing right here when Stevie threw the hat down," said Collette slowly. Maybe if she replayed the entire scene, step by step, she would remember where the hat dropped. Maybe the ring was in the grass.

"Did you drop the hat?" asked Kicky. "When you first grabbed it from Stevie."

Collette shook her head. "No. I held it, and then Stevie wanted it back, and then . . ." Collette stopped, trying to think of what had happened next. Jeff had scared Stevie by saying that Mom was going to kill him, and then Kicky had offered to take the hat inside. Collette glanced up and studied Kicky's face. Kicky had held the hat last. She was the last one to see the ring.

"Collette, what's wrong?" asked Jeff.

"Aunt Helen's ring is missing. It's not on the hat anymore." Collette bent down and raked her fingers through the grass.

"Stevie threw it down and you picked it up, Collette," reminded Jeff. "Was the ring on then?"

"I guess." Collette stood up. "I think it was."

"Well, who else touched the hat?" Jeff asked. "Did one of those little campers play with it?"

"Of course not." Collette was a little insulted that Jeff would think she would give something so valuable to a kid. "Kicky offered to take the hat into the house, remember?"

Kicky nodded. "I was trying to help."

"I know, I know. That was helping." Collette stopped, thinking. "I was just wondering if maybe you dropped the hat. Maybe the ring fell off then."

"I didn't drop it," said Kicky. "You saw me with the hat. You saw me the whole time."

Collette nodded. "Yes, well . . . except when you were up on the porch. I didn't see you then." Collette drew in a shaky breath. "Did you try on some of the jewelry?"

153

Kicky's cheeks blazed red. "What's *that* supposed to mean?"

Collette shook her head. "Nothing, I just wondered if maybe you dropped it or something. . . ."

Kicky's face hardened. "Yeah — *or something.* I know what you mean by that. Boy, Collette, one minute you are so nice to me it's almost phony and the next you — "

"Kicky. I wasn't accusing you."

Kicky took a step toward Collette. "Sounded that way to me. You're just like everyone else, Collette. You're nice to me for ten minutes and then you're mean. I didn't take your stupid, stupid ring. Just 'cause I'm a foster kid doesn't mean I steal."

"It doesn't mean you *don't* steal, either," said Jeff. "Where's the ring?"

Kicky spun around. "How should I know? I'm not in charge of this *dumb* camp!"

"It's not dumb," shouted Jeff. "You had the ring last."

Collette pushed herself between the two. "Stop all the yelling."

Roger turned off his music and ran over. "What's wrong?"

154

The holiday hat parade came to a halt.

"Listen, Jeff, Kicky was trying to help me *find* the ring," said Collette in a forceful whisper. "If you both don't be quiet, Mom is going to come running out here to see what's going on."

"Good, let her," said Kicky. She crossed her arms and glared at Jeff. "Your mother is a nice lady. She will tell this kid to mind his own business."

"No, sir. My mom will stick up for *me*. And, she really liked that ring!"

"Jeff," warned Collette. "I'm in charge so be quiet. After camp we'll all look for the ring."

"I don't have to," grumbled Kicky.

"Course not, Kicky," muttered Jeff. "That's 'cause the ring's in your pocket."

Kicky swung her foot back and whacked Jeff in the shin.

"Stop it, Kicky." Collette pushed her away from Jeff.

"Yeow!" cried Jeff, hopping backward on one leg. "You're not allowed to hit at camp." Jeff rubbed his shin. "You don't even live in our neighborhood so you aren't even really allowed in this camp at all."

Collette saw the flash of pure pain in Kicky's eyes.

"Well *being* here sure isn't my idea," said Kicky.

"Stop it!" hissed Collette. "Jeff, you don't know that Kicky took the ring. I mean, it probably just fell off the hat." Collette tried to give Kicky a quick smile. But Kicky's stone face bounced Collette's smile right back.

"Come on, Eddie," said Kicky quietly. "We're going *home*."

"You can't," said Collette quickly. "It's not even ten o'clock and Mrs. Lister may not be home. I'm in charge of you two until noon."

Kicky just grunted. "You aren't a bit in charge of me. I said I was going *home*." Kicky started to pull Eddie down the driveway. "Eddie and I are sick of all this."

Collette hurried down the drive after Kicky and Eddie. "Wait a minute, Kicky. Jeff didn't mean what he said about you guys not belonging. He's mad. And . . . if we all help look for the ring, I know we'll be able to find it."

"Who cares?" muttered Kicky. "Just because I don't have a fancy ring like that doesn't mean I even want one."

"Momma would like a ring like that," said Eddie softly. "I wish I had that ring."

Kicky tugged on his arm. "Be quiet, Eddie. You want these dumb kids thinking *you* took the ring?"

Eddie shook his head.

"Stay, please," begged Collette.

Eddie pulled on Kicky's arm. "Let's stay, Kicky. I like it here."

"Hey, where are you guys going?" asked Roger. "The hat contest is over and I was just about to start the scavenger hunt. I need you two to help me."

"Yippee!" cried Eddie. He hugged Kicky. "Come on, Kicky. You can help me win a prize."

Kicky rubbed her hand over her eyes. Collette felt an ache in her heart. Kicky looked so old and worn out.

Kicky looked down at Eddie. "Okay, Eddie. You can stay for the scavenger hunt. But I don't want us to come back here tomorrow." Kicky looked up at Collette. "If a pretzel is missing, they'll think we stole it."

"Kicky, I never said you took the ring. It's just

gone, that's all." Collette tried to smile. "Who won the happy hat contest, Eddie?"

"Ginger. She stuck Lifesavers all over her hat."

Collette turned around and smiled at Kicky. She wanted her to feel included, too. "Kicky, do you want to help Roger and me explain the scavenger hunt to the campers?"

"No." Kicky sat down on the bottom step. "I'm not getting paid to be a counselor. I'm the thief, remember?"

"Oh, Kicky," groaned Collette. "Stop feeling sorry for yourself. I'm going to help Marsha and Roger get started, and then I'm going to look for the ring, okay? I'm sure it's in the grass. Nobody is a thief!"

Eddie smiled. "That's good. I hope you find it. Hey, Collette, your mom's on the porch. Maybe she can help you look."

"Oh, wait, Eddie," Collette said quickly. She bent down and whispered close to his ear. "In fact, we won't tell her because she might get worried and then she won't feel too hot. We'll tell her after we find the ring."

"Okay," said Eddie. "I'm going to run inside and go to the bathroom."

158

Collette hurried after him. She better make sure Eddie didn't accidentally tell her mother that the ruby ring was missing.

"Hi, Mrs. Murphy," Eddie called out as he rushed by. "Roger is taking us on a scavenger hunt."

"Sounds like fun, Eddie," said Mrs. Murphy.

"Hi, Mom," said Collette. "Why are you leaning against the wall like that?" Mrs. Murphy didn't look a bit comfortable.

"My back is killing me and, when I sit down, my stomach hurts." Mrs. Murphy gave a tired laugh. "So the only way I feel halfway all right is by leaning against the wall."

Collette sat on the bottom step. "Do you want a hot water bottle or something? Should I call Daddy?"

Mrs. Murphy shook her head. "I'm okay. I guess I forgot what it feels like to be so pregnant."

Eddie rushed back out, slamming the screen door. "Let's get going, Collette."

"Hurry, Eddie," called Collette. "They're all lined up."

"Where's Stevie?" asked Mrs. Murphy. "Doesn't he want to go?"

Eddie turned and shrugged his shoulders. "I couldn't find Stevie."

"He's probably already with Roger and Marsha," said Collette. "Everyone is excited about the scavenger hunt."

Mrs. Murphy stood up and peered across the yard. "He needs some more sunscreen. I better go get him."

Mrs. Murphy started down the first step and froze. Her eyes opened wide and Collette saw her knuckles grow white as she gripped the banister.

"What's wrong, Mom?"

Mrs. Murphy didn't speak for a second, then she slowly slid down to the first step. "Oh, gosh. I really don't feel too well."

"Are you okay, Mom?" Collette asked again.

Mrs. Murphy nodded, then drew in a deep breath and let it out slowly. "Sure. I guess I just stayed on my feet too long today. I'm going back inside. I'll call Marsha's mom and ask her to come over."

Collette walked over to the large group of campers lined up around the picnic table. Roger was busy explaining what a scavenger hunt was, while Marsha passed out pictures of the items they needed to find. Collette leaned down and looked at Wilbur's page. Marsha had cut items out of the magazine and pasted them on the paper: a rock, a feather, lots of leaves. Even the little kids who couldn't read would be able to understand.

"This is cool!" cried Wilbur. "Hey, Eddie, do you want to be my partner?"

"Kicky will be my partner," said Eddie. "She's real smart." Eddie turned around. "Hey, where is Kicky?"

"Check the stairs, Eddie." Collette studied Wilbur's page. Suddenly, she smiled. "Hey, kids. I want to add one more thing to your scavenger list."

Marsha looked worried. "It's a little late for that, Collette."

"A red ruby ring," explained Collette. "I think it's in the grass near the porch. Whoever finds it will get an extra prize."

Roger and Marsha nodded. "We'll help them look."

"It fell off the hat accidentally," added Collette. She hoped Kicky had heard. Kicky had to know that Collette didn't really believe she took the ring, now.

Collette's gaze swept the circle, counting the campers. "Eight, nine, ten, Laura and Jeff make twelve, Eddie's thirteen and . . ." Collette peered around to the side yard, looking for Stevie.

"Where's Kicky?" asked Eddie again as he ran back across the yard. "She's not on the stairs and she's not anywhere."

Collette's head swung from the empty stone wall, to the empty steps, to the dark garage. She couldn't see Kicky or Stevie.

"The garage door's half open, Eddie," said Collette. "Let's go see if they're inside, trying to stay cool."

Collette didn't even believe herself as she walked across the driveway. Before she was half-way there, her heart began to pound. She lifted the creaking white door and peered inside. Nobody was there. Laura's little nurse desk and chair were empty.

"Not here," cried Eddie. "Kicky is always supposed to watch me. Momma said."

Collette flicked on the garage light and looked around the room once more. That's when she noticed Stevie's tiny fire-engine-red bike was missing.

Chapter Seventeen

"Stevie's gone," whispered Collette.

"Did he run away?" asked Eddie.

"I hope not," Collette said softly. "Maybe he's just riding his bicycle on the street." Collette tried hard to make herself believe it, too. "I'll ask Jeff to go look."

"Is Kicky with Stevie?" asked Eddie. "Kicky's not anywhere in the yard. Can Jeff look for Kicky, too?"

Collette squeezed Eddie's hand. "I'll look."

"Kicky told me she would *never* leave me," added Eddie quietly. "She promised."

Collette felt chills race up both arms. What if Kicky and Stevie had both run away? As Collette walked quickly out of the garage, a small voice inside her began to nag. *"Well, what did you expect Kicky and Stevie to do? Of course they ran away."*

"Eddie, go stay with Roger and the others. I'll find Kicky and Stevie and be right back."

"Okay," agreed Eddie slowly. "But find Kicky right away."

Collette hurried down the driveway and looked up and down Browning Road. Aside from Mrs. Yurkon's little brown dog, the street was empty.

"Keep calm, keep calm," Collette reminded herself. "You can't spaz out and scare the campers half to death. And you certainly can't tell Mom. News like this would make her faint." Collette raced back up the driveway and walked quickly over to Roger.

"Where's Kicky?" asked Eddie. "Did you find her yet?"

"I'm still looking," Collette said. She smiled at Eddie until he turned away, then she grabbed onto Roger's arm. "Hey, Rog, have you seen Stevie and Kicky? I can't find them anywhere."

"They may be inside," said Roger. "It's pretty hot out here. Kicky is always hanging around your mom." Roger blasted his whistle. "Come on, guys. Everyone make sure you have a partner. Make sure you have your chart, too. Remember, the first one who finds everything on their page is the winner."

"And there's an extra prize if you find the ruby ring," added Marsha as she held up a large pink dog. "An extra bonus prize."

"Yippee!" cried the campers. "Let's get started."

"Ready, guys?" called out Roger.

Collette tugged on Roger's arm. "Stevie isn't inside, Roger," explained Collette. She was having a hard time breathing and an even harder time keeping calm. She wanted to just scream! "His bike is missing, too. And I think Kicky got mad because she thinks we think she took the ring and . . ."

"They are probably on the street," said Roger calmly. "Relax, Collette. Now let go of my arm because I've got to get started. These kids are ready to go. Jeff, get the kids out of the sandbox and back in line."

Jeff! Collette bolted to the sandbox. "Jeff, come here, quick. I have to talk to you."

Jeff brushed sand from Wilbur's knees. "Go get back in line."

"Jeff, Stevie is gone. He's not in the house or the yard. And Kicky's missing, too."

"So?"

"So? So I heard you accuse Kicky. And what did you say to Stevie when I went into the house?"

"Nothing." Jeff shoved his hands in his pockets. "You can't blame me for this, Collette. It's your fault, too. You're the one in charge!"

"Jeff, I am not *blaming* you," whispered Collette. She glanced over her shoulder, hoping her mother wasn't back on the porch. "Tell me the truth. Did you say something else to scare him? We have to find him before Mom notices he's gone."

Jeff was beginning to look worried, too. "Stevie shouldn't have taken Mom's good jewelry."

"I know. But, tell me exactly what else you said to Stevie." Collette was trying her hardest to stay calm. "I won't get mad, I promise."

Jeff looked down at his shoes. "I didn't think he would *believe* me." When he looked up, he was so pale, his freckles practically jumped off his face. "I just said he . . ." Jeff swallowed. "He might

166

. . . might be a hundred years old when they let him out of jail. That's all."

Collette sighed. "That's *enough* . . . Holy cow, Jeff. Stevie didn't lose the ring on purpose. He's only five years old . . ."

Jeff yanked his baseball hat down over his eyes. "You're the one who's supposed to be in charge of this camp, Collette. Not me."

Collette closed her eyes. Why had she *ever* wanted to be in charge?

"What's going on?" Marsha stood next to Collette. "Roger said Kicky and Stevie disappeared."

"I think maybe Kicky and Stevie ran away," said Collette.

"Maybe Kicky kidnapped Stevie," suggested Jeff.

"Jeff!" cried Collette.

"Well, she hates our guts now," said Jeff. "And we still don't have the ring."

"Guys," whispered Marsha. "I know you have a major emergency, but Roger said we have to get going. He can't make the kids stand in line anymore. We'll help you look as soon as the scavenger hunt is over. Just keep searching until then."

Tears stung Collette's eyes. She was going to

167

have to tell her mother. Marsha's mother would be arriving any minute to help.

Collette glanced up at the kitchen window. She hated the idea of one more secret she had to keep from her mother. But if she walked in and announced Stevie was missing, her mother would start running up and down the street looking for him. All that running would be bad for the baby.

Collette wasn't sure when a baby was exactly finished, but she didn't want to risk it.

Collette closed her eyes. "Oh, please, God. Help me find them. I know I messed up with Kicky and totally ignored Stevie. But, please help me find them before they get hurt."

Marsha jiggled her arm. "Are you okay?"

Collette bit her lip and blinked fast. If she started crying, she may not be able to stop. Why hadn't she talked to Stevie right away to let him know that he hadn't done anything wrong on purpose? Why hadn't she treated Kicky just like the other campers, instead of some special project?

"Okay, listen, Collette," said Marsha. "Keep calm and you and Jeff go look for Stevie and Kicky. Roger and I will help you right after the scavenger hunt. They're probably just taking a walk."

"Thanks, Marsha." Collette couldn't even pretend to believe it.

"Then, we'll start the next activity. We have at least two more hours before the parents come." Marsha peered at Collette's clipboard. "What's next?"

Collette glanced down at her clipboard. Everything was a blur. The only activity that really seemed important now was finding Stevie and Kicky.

"Everyone takes off their shoes and walks around the yard," explained Collette. "Then they take everything that has stuck to their socks and they paste it on paper to make a picture. It's called a Fuz — " Collette's voice cracked. "It's called a Fuzzy-Wuzzy Walk." Stevie had named it last night when Collette told him about the activity.

Marsha patted Collette on the back. "You'll find them. But hurry up."

"If I don't find them in five minutes, we'll have to tell your mom," said Collette. She grabbed Jeff's hand. "Come on, Jeff."

Collette and Jeff walked carefully across the yard. "Smile when you pass the kitchen window in case Mom is looking out," said Collette. "Try to look normal."

As soon as they cleared the house, they both sped down the driveway and headed up Browning Road. Collette looked to the left and right for Stevie's red bike. Jeff raced up ahead, calling Stevie's name as quietly as he could.

"Please, God," whispered Collette. "If You find them, I'll never ask for another thing in my whole life."

Collette was just about to add, "This time I mean it," when she saw Kicky sitting under a shade tree in Mrs. Yurkon's side yard, petting a small brown dog.

Collette was so stunned she couldn't move for a second, and then so relieved, she started to cry.

"What's wrong with you?" asked Kicky. "Lose some more jewelry?"

"No, I found you," said Collette.

Kicky frowned. "Who said I was lost? I was sick of being where I wasn't wanted. I decided to wait for Eddie here. I'm never lost."

Collette sighed and walked over. "I thought you were. And I can't find Stevie, either."

Kicky shook her head. "Some camp you're running. You don't even know what you're doing. You shouldn't be in charge."

Collette leaned against the tree, feeling weaker and more confused than ever. "You're right," she said quietly. "I've messed everything up. I don't know what I'm doing at all."

"So stop crying and get in charge," said Kicky. "Do something."

Collette drew in a deep breath. "Okay. The first thing on my new list is to find Stevie." Collette stood up. "In fact, it's the *only* thing."

Chapter Eighteen

"So when did you see Stevie last?" asked Kicky. She was on her feet now, heading toward the sidewalk.

"Right after we took his hat away."

Kicky grunted. "Yeah, right after your dumb brother and you asked me if I stole the ring."

"Kicky, I'm sorry." Collette's voice cracked. "I thought you ran away, too."

Kicky shot Collette a disgusted look. "Me? Run away? Hey, you guys got me mad, but I'd *never* leave without Eddie." Kicky's cheeks flashed red. "You don't know too much about little brothers, do you?"

Collette bit her lip so she wouldn't start crying

again. She didn't know too much about *anything* right now. Why did she think taking care of kids would be as easy as writing down activities on a plastic clipboard? "I'm a crummy big sister. I feel sorry for the new baby."

"Hey, hey," said Kicky. "I just meant that I would never run out on my little brother like that. I wasn't trying to insult you. You're not *that* bad."

Collette shook her head. "No, I deserved it. Stevie's gone. What if I can't find him?"

"He's probably in the house," said Kicky. "A kid would have to be nuts to run away from your mom. She's so nice."

Collette felt a chill race down her back at the mention of her mother. "Stevie didn't run away from my mom. He ran away from me and Jeff. He thinks he's going to jail for losing my mom's ring."

"All this junk going on, just because of a silly ring," Kicky said angrily. "Aunt Helen's probably dead. She doesn't care."

"I know. *I* don't even care about the ring now. I just want to find Stevie." Collette started walking faster. "I can't believe he just ran away. Eddie would never do that to you, Kicky."

"Eddie and I have to stick together."

"You're such a great sister, Kicky." Collette could hear the jealousy in her own voice.

"Sometimes. Sometimes I make dumb choices for Eddie. Like when I made him run away from those other foster homes." Kicky nudged Collette with her elbow. "No sister is perfect all of the time. Come on, let's start looking."

"Thanks." Collette saw Jeff two yards over. He was still alone.

"Hey, you found Kicky," cried Jeff. He cut through a side hedge and ran over. "That's good."

"I was never lost," answered Kicky.

"I guess you didn't find Stevie." Collette said.

Jeff shook his head. "We better call Dad, Collette."

"I know." Collette cupped her hands and called Stevie's name one last time. "Stevie Murphy!"

Kicky pulled Collette's hands down. "Shhhhhh, holy cow, Collette. Your mom will hear you. And Stevie will hide."

"She's going to know anyway," said Collette. "We can't keep this a secret anymore."

"Where's Stevie's favorite spot?" asked Kicky. Her voice sounded as calm as a detective's.

"Disney World," said Jeff.

Kicky groaned. "On the *street*. Where does he like to hang out?"

Collette and Jeff looked at each other and shrugged. Collette felt guilty all over again, realizing how little she knew about her brother. Kicky probably knew *everything* about Eddie.

"He likes to play in the dirt by the shade trees near Marsha's yard," said Jeff. "He takes his little G.I. Joes there."

"Good. You go look there, Jeff," said Kicky. "And if he tries to run, you better catch him."

"Okay," Jeff raced back down the street.

Collette felt her heart pounding. Would Stevie really try to escape from his own family? Did he really think she cared more about a ruby ring than about him?

"I'm so scared," said Collette.

"Being scared isn't going to find your brother," snapped Kicky.

"I know."

"Now, think," ordered Kicky. "Hasn't Stevie ever come home, all happy and dirty and told you he had a great time somewhere on this street?"

Collette shook her head. She couldn't remember. Stevie was a little kid who had a great time everywhere. "Why does it have to be a great time place?" asked Collette. "If you're running away, don't you just want a place you can't be found?"

Kicky looked sad all of a sudden. "No," she said quietly. "If you're hurting enough to run away, then all you want is a place that will make you feel happy again."

She pulled Collette up the street. "Now, try to remember. Where does that kid have the most fun? Where did you go for fun on the street?"

Collette walked to the edge of the sidewalk, and looked up and down the street. She glanced at the tree swing hanging in the Cillos' backyard, the stone wall at the very end of the dead-end street, the house with the new puppies, and . . .

"The cat lady's house!" cried Collette. She turned and smiled at Kicky.

"Who is the cat lady?" asked Kicky.

"I'll show you. Come on," cried Collette. "Stevie loves Mrs. White. At first he thought she was a witch, but then he got to know her and now he goes there a lot."

"Great," said Kicky. She grinned and punched

Collette lightly in the shoulder. "See, you aren't such a crummy sister, after all. You know your little brother, just like I know Eddie."

Collette returned a worried smile, hoping Kicky was right.

Chapter Nineteen

As they stood in front of the cat lady's dark, three-story house, Kicky's mouth fell open.

"Holy cow! She *must* be a witch."

Collette pushed open the black wrought-iron gate and smiled. "She's really nice. She's an artist and lives here with twelve or thirteen cats."

"Does she eat them?" giggled Kicky.

Collette turned quickly, staring at Kicky. "How did you know?"

"Know what?"

"That's what all the neighborhood kids always thought."

Kicky shrugged. "This house looks creepy. Why

are the shutters closed on the third floor? Is anyone up there?"

Collette closed her mouth before she could say anything else. *Like, wow, when you aren't being Eddie's guardian angel, you do think like a kid after all.*

Collette rang the chimed brass bell, and when Mrs. White didn't answer, she used the heavy knocker.

"Maybe he isn't here," said Kicky.

Collette hopped over the side of the railing. "Let's look in the back." Collette peered into the holly bushes and rosebushes growing along the side of the house. If Stevie wasn't here, where could he be?

Kicky grabbed hold of Collette's arm. "Hey, what's that over there by the garage?"

Leaning against the bricks was Stevie's red tricycle.

"Stevie!" cried Collette, running into the backyard. "Stevie, where are you?"

"He's not here," came a high squeaky voice. "I'm Mrs. White and you better get out of here before my cats eat you up."

Kicky grabbed Collette's arm. "Who's that?"

"I'm a witch," the squeaky voice answered.

Collette started to laugh, covering her mouth. She pointed to the garage doors. One was opened halfway, held up by a short stack of bricks. "Stevie," Collette whispered.

"Mrs. White, have you seen Stevie?"

"I ate him up," came the squeaky voice. "So you better leave. I'm still hungry."

"That's too bad," said Collette. She stopped smiling. It really wasn't funny when you thought of it. Stevie would rather be in a dark, gloomy garage instead of having fun at his big sister's camp.

"I came to tell Stevie I was sorry I yelled at him."

"Is that bad Jeff sorry?" asked the voice.

"Jeff's real sorry," Collette added. "He's worried and running up and down the street looking for Stevie."

"Jeff's a wimp," announced the squeaky voice. "Jeff said I was a dumb-head."

"Can you give me back Stevie?" asked Collette.

"Stevie's all chewed up."

"Kicky, this might take a while," whispered Collette. "Can you run back to camp and tell Roger and Marsha that I'll be there as soon as I can? Tell Jeff that . . ."

"You can give Jeff the message," said Kicky. "I'm not speaking to him."

"Tell me what? What's wrong?"

Collette looked up. Jeff was standing in the driveway, puffing and looking scared.

"Stevie's okay," said Collette quickly. "He's in the garage."

"No, sir," came the squeaky voice.

Jeff barely glanced at the garage. He took a deep breath and rubbed his forehead. "Good, but . . . , oh, man!" He took another deep breath. "Collette, you better run back home. An ambulance is on the way."

"What?" cried Kicky and Collette at once.

"What happened, Jeff?" asked Collette. She had left Roger and Marsha in charge!

Stevie scurried out of the garage. "Who got hurt?"

"Is Eddie okay?" asked Kicky. "Jeff, is Eddie all right?"

Jeff nodded, speaking so fast you could barely understand him. "Yeah, Eddie's fine. All the kids are fine? But . . ."

"Why is the ambulance coming then?" cried Collette. She was so scared she was practically screaming. "Tell me, Jeff!"

"It's Mom," Jeff blurted out, "The ambulance is coming for Mom!"

Chapter Twenty

"What's wrong with Mom?" cried Collette.

"Nothing bad," Jeff shouted back over his shoulder. "The baby's coming!"

"Mom's having the baby!" Collette let out a shout and hugged Kicky. "I'm so excited!"

"Can I ride in the ambulance?" asked Stevie, hopping on his tricycle. "Hey, Jeff, tell them guys to wait for me."

Kicky looked worried. "Is it okay for her to have the baby today? I mean, your mom told me she was supposed to have it in a couple of weeks."

Collette shrugged. "I guess no one told the baby." She turned around and smiled at Stevie.

"Come on, Stevie. Ride your bike home as fast as you can."

Stevie nodded, then stopped pedaling. "Hey, wait a minute. I *can't* go home yet. I didn't find Mommy's ring. I don't want her to be mad at me."

"Mommy doesn't even *know* about the ring," insisted Collette. "She's busy having the baby."

"Hurry!" yelled Jeff from the end of the driveway.

Stevie, Kicky, and Collette flew down the street after Jeff. As she ran, Collette tried hard to decide if she should be excited that the baby was finally coming, or worried that an ambulance had to take her mother to the hospital. In the movies, couples always called a taxi.

The ambulance was parked in front of the Murphy house, its red lights flashing. Neighbors were coming outside, and the entire summer camp was standing in the front yard. Marsha, Roger, and Mrs. Cessano were holding as many hands as they could.

"There's your mom," said Kicky.

"Holy cow!" cried Collette. She stared as a lady and a man carried a stretcher slowly down the front steps. A white sheet covered Mrs. Murphy.

184

"Is Mommy going to have the baby outside?" asked Stevie. "In the yard?"

"They're taking her to the hospital," said Collette. She ran up and waited at the bottom of the stairs. "Mom, are you okay?"

Mrs. Murphy nodded. "Yes, fine. Looks like our baby is on the way."

"Stand back, honey," said the female paramedic. "Your mom's going to have this baby right on the sidewalk unless we hurry."

"Cool!" cried Stevie. "Hi, Mommy. I didn't run away or get eaten up by the cat lady, and your ring isn't really losted, but . . ."

Collette quickly put her hand over Stevie's mouth. But Mrs. Murphy started her breathing and looked so busy that Collette was sure she didn't hear a word.

"Don't worry about a thing, Kate," Mrs. Cessano called out. "I called your husband and he's meeting you at the hospital. I'll watch the kids."

"Bye, Mom. I love you," Collette called out as her mother disappeared into the ambulance. "Don't worry. I'll watch the kids, too."

"Good luck, Mrs. Murphy," called Kicky.

"Bye!" shouted the campers.

"Good luck, Kate!" The neighbors cried. Mrs. Yurkon raised her coffee cup and Mr. Nassar turned off his mower and waved his baseball cap as the ambulance backed into the driveway and then sped off down Browning Road.

Everyone started cheering and talking at once. A few ladies hurried over to talk to Mrs. Cessano, promising to bring cake and fried chicken over. Mr. Nassar promised Jeff that the Murphy lawn would be cut as soon as he finished his.

"Wow," said Kicky, looking around at the busy excitement going on in the Murphys' front yard. "Everyone is acting like it's the Fourth of July."

Collette started to laugh. "A new baby's on the way," she said. "Everyone loves babies."

Kicky looked around the yard. "I better go get Eddie. He doesn't know where I am."

"Collette!" Laura raced down the yard and straight into Collette's arms. "I got to be the nurse lady for Mommy. She told me to call 911!"

"Good work, Laura." Collette hugged her sister back.

"And Mrs. Cessano said we can all wait up till the baby pops out, even if it's midnight! But Marsha's mom said the baby will probably be here in two minutes."

"We may have a little sister soon," laughed Collette.

"A brother," laughed Jeff from the front porch.

Collette glanced over at Kicky, who was busy hugging Eddie. She walked over. "Your sister helped me find Stevie, Eddie," said Collette. "She was a big help."

"Kicky's smart," said Eddie. "But, I found something, too."

"What?" asked Collette, kneeling down. "Did you win the scavenger hunt? Let me see."

Eddie dug deep in his pocket. "Better than that!" He pulled out Aunt Helen's ring. "The ring! I found it right on the back porch. Next to the milk carton box! I showed Marsha and she hugged me."

Kicky and Collette both started to laugh. "Holy cow!" laughed Collette. "You and your sister are the best detectives in the neighborhood!" Collette took the ring and held it up. "Hey, Stevie and Jeff, look. Eddie found the ring!"

"Here's *my* hug," laughed Collette. "Thanks, Eddie!"

Marsha came racing around the side of the house, the large pink dog high over her head. "First prize goes to Eddie!"

Roger grabbed the pink dog from Marsha and tossed it across the yard to Kicky. "Catch."

Kicky caught it and smiled. "Congratulations, Eddie." She bent down and handed him the dog. "I'm proud of you."

Eddie pushed the dog back toward Kicky. "You can keep it, Kicky. I won it for you!"

"Just what I need," laughed Kicky. "Someone else to be in charge of."

"Let's get in the backyard, campers," called out Mrs. Cessano. "Roger, Marsha, Collette. Lend a hand. It's snack time!"

Collette herded the Lister boys and the Cillo sisters down the side steps to the driveway. "Kicky, my dad will be calling us to tell us about the baby soon. Would you and Eddie want to wait with us after camp?" asked Collette. "It will be like a party."

Kicky looked surprised. "You mean you want us to stay once camp is over? Mikey and Matt, too. They're okay once they know who's boss."

"If it's all right with Mrs. Lister. Marsha will be

here, and I'll ask Roger to stay, too." Collette held up the ring. "I might need you to help me keep this safe."

Laura ran over and grabbed Kicky's hand. "Say yes."

"Sure," said Kicky slowly. "If you really want us to."

"I do," said Collette. "I'm so nervous. I really need you around."

"In case you lose another kid?" asked Kicky. She smiled.

"Yeah," Collette said, grinning back. "I've just elected you head counselor. In charge of me."

Chapter Twenty-one

"Collette, when are they going to call?" asked Laura for the one hundredth time. "We've been waiting for too long."

"It will be soon," answered Mrs. Cessano cheerfully. "You can't rush a baby." She set a plate of brownies down in the center of the Murphy table. "Mrs. Cillo sent these down. They're still warm."

"I hope it's a girl," said Collette wistfully. Marsha, Kicky, and she had been at the kitchen table for almost an hour, making list after list of girl's names. Roger had stayed for thirty minutes, and then wanted to go visit John and tell him all about camp.

"I like Karen Kimberly the best," said Kicky.

She bit into a brownie and made a chocolate face for Eddie.

"Gross!" laughed Eddie. He walked his G.I. Joe over to the brownie plate and took a square. "You just like Karen 'cause that's your name."

"Is Karen your real name?" Collette and Marsha both asked together.

Kicky nodded. "Yeah, well Kicky is more me."

Jeff snorted. "You can say that again."

"I think she should be named Marsha, after me," suggested Marsha. "Marsha Murphy."

"How about naming the baby Roger?" giggled Kicky.

Marsha's eyes bugged out. "How did you know that kid drives me nuts?" Marsha blew her bangs straight up. "Trust me, Kicky. Roger was normal as a counselor, but he has been crazy as a loon since kindergarten. The creep stuck a dead snake in my locker last year."

"He's funny," said Kicky. "I like him."

Collette nodded. "I like him, too." Collette added the name Karen Kimberly to her list of girl's names. She slid her paper toward Kicky so she could see.

Kicky didn't say anything, but her cheeks grew

pink and Collette could see the smile she was trying to hide.

"Here, Eddie," said Stevie, pushing two more G.I. Joes across the table. "You can keep all these guys."

"Wow," said Matt.

"To take home?" Eddie's eyes lit up. "For forever?"

"Yeah, I got lots. Boy, am I glad you found that ring."

"Can we have some?" asked Mikey. "Since I'm being good?"

"Sure."

"Hey, Stevie," said Collette. "When Mom has this baby, then you'll be a big brother."

"I know that." Stevie's G.I. Joe stuck his foot in a brownie. "Help, I in quicksand!"

"Will you be jealous?" asked Kicky. "You won't be the youngest any more."

Stevie shrugged, smashing a little bit of brownie into his G.I. Joe's face. "No. A baby will be fun."

Jeff slid into a kitchen chair. "Stevie, stop messing up the brownies. Save some for Dad."

Stevie nodded, shoving the rest of the brownie into his mouth.

Collette glanced at the clock. Waiting for a baby took such a long time.

"Mrs. Cessano, I thought you said the baby was going to be here in two minutes," said Collette.

"I was joking. Your mother went into labor so fast it scared me to death." Mrs. Cessano put her hand on Marsha's shiny black hair. "I still remember when I had Marsha. I was in labor for twelve hours."

Marsha batted her eyelashes. "But of course I was worth every minute. I was a perfect, perfect baby."

"What happened?" Jeff asked quietly. He tried to hide his smile.

"Jeff!" Marsha shot a chunk of brownie across the table.

"Marsha!" warned Mrs. Cessano. "Stop it. You are a guest in this house."

Kicky and Collette caught each other's eyes and smiled.

"I'm calling the hospital," announced Jeff. "I bet that baby is already here. Dad probably ordered pizza to celebrate and they forgot to call us."

Mrs. Cessano put her hand on the phone. "No,

Jeff. Be patient. Your father said he would call as soon as — "

The phone rang beneath Mrs. Cessano's hand. Everyone jumped. It rang again.

"Who wants to answer it?" asked Mrs. Cessano cheerfully.

"Collette!" Kicky said quickly. "She's the big sister."

"No fair," muttered Stevie, dipping his G.I. Joe into Jeff's milk. "Helpppppp! I drowning."

As the phone rang for the third time, Collette grabbed it.

"Hello?"

"Peanut!" Her father sounded so happy. "Hey, I've got good news."

"Mom had the baby!" Collette cried. She felt chills racing up and down her back. The baby, at last.

Everyone hopped up from the chairs and gathered around Collette. "Is it a baby sister?" asked Collette. She could hardly wait to dress it in a pink little dress with matching booties.

"No. No sister this time," Mr. Murphy laughed.

"A boy!" cried Collette. A little brother would be wonderful. They could buy him a tiny little baseball glove and bat. "That's great, Daddy! Another little brother!"

"Hurrah!" Jeff and Stevie slapped each other a high five. "The boys are winning!"

"Another *boy*?" groaned Marsha. "Just don't name him Roger."

"Now we have three boys!" said Collette.

"No, not *really*," laughed Mr. Murphy.

Collette pressed the phone closer to her ear. The kitchen was so noisy she could barely hear her father. "What did you say?"

"I said we didn't have a boy," Mr. Murphy shouted back.

"Mom had a girl?" cried Collette. She held the phone to her chest and turned to the group. "Hey, we don't have a brother, we have a sister!"

Laura, Kicky, and Marsha started to cheer. Stevie crossed his arms and frowned.

"No fair. Now we can't name the baby G.I. Joey."

"Is she cute, Daddy?" asked Collette.

"No sisters this time," repeated Mr. Murphy.

"Daddy!" Collette cried. "Stop teasing. If it isn't a boy and it isn't a girl, what is it?"

"A puppy!" cried Stevie. "Yipeeeee!"

Mr. Murphy laughed for a long time on the other end of the phone. "Sorry to tease, Peanut. Mom didn't have a girl or a boy. Your mother just had twins!"

"Twins?" Collette's voice squeaked.

"Twins?" cried Mrs. Cessano. She slid down onto a kitchen chair.

"Two healthy, beautiful boys," continued Mr. Murphy. "Surprised us all. Even the doctor."

"Twin boys," repeated Collette. She started smiling from ear to ear. She felt Kicky's hand on her shoulder. Jeff grabbed the phone and started talking a mile a minute. Stevie, Eddie, and the Lister boys began running through the house, screaming, "We won, the boys won."

Mrs. Cessano hopped up from her chair. "Excuse me, kids. I'm going to tell the neighbors. They will *never* believe this."

"I'll help you tell everyone," offered Laura as she followed Mrs. Cessano out the back door. "Now Collette and I will each have a baby to hold."

"*Twin* brothers," Marsha whistled and shook her head. "You're so lucky, Collette."

"Two more babies," whispered Collette. "I'm the big sister to five kids. Wow . . ."

Kicky gave Collette a light punch in the arm. "Hey, wake up, lady. You're happy, aren't you?"

Collette nodded, then shook her head. "Yeah, sure. But . . . what if my mom has to run to the store and leaves me in charge? Gosh, after doing such a crummy job as a counselor, how am I ever going to be a good big sister to so many kids?"

"Who said you were a crummy counselor?" said Marsha. "I think you were great." Marsha grinned. "Almost as good as me."

Collette nodded. It was nice to hear, but she sure hadn't been great with Kicky or Stevie. Camp Summer Fun was supposed to be their best week, not their worst.

"I think you're a good sister," said Kicky.

Collette's head jerked up. Kicky looked like she meant what she was saying.

"Not as good as you," Collette said honestly. "You are the best big sister I've ever seen."

"Thanks," said Kicky. "I try to be. I guess I *have* to be. For Eddie, until we get back home. I promised my mom."

"I hope you get to go home soon," Collette said.

"Me, too," added Marsha.

Kicky nodded. "Thanks. Eddie and I stick together. We have a lot of glue between us. That's mostly what a big sister does. Makes sure the glue is still there." Kicky nudged Collette. "Get it — sticking — glue."

Collette laughed. "I hope I have enough glue for twins."

"We better get busy finding names for them," pointed out Marsha.

Collette and Kicky sat down and picked up their pencils.

"I guess we can forget Karen Kimberly," said Kicky. "Your brothers wouldn't appreciate it."

"Bradley James," announced Collette.

"Joseph Michael," suggested Kicky.

"John McKechnie the second," giggled Marsha. "Just in case John McKechnie the first never speaks to me again."

A loud crash and a thump came from upstairs. Collette stood up and ran to the bottom of the stairs. "What broke?"

The stairwell was silent for a second, then Stevie stuck his curly blond head over the banister. "Collette, is the brown lamp in Mommy's room old?"

"Stevie," said Collette in a low voice. "Did you break it?"

"Just a little."

Collette started up the stairs. Stevie was always breaking things. He never meant to get in trouble; he just seemed to attract it, like a magnet.

"Collette, don't worry because I bet you can fix it!" cried Stevie. He held up two large sections of her mother's brown ginger jar lamp. "All you have to do is glue it." Stevie smiled. "That's all. Do you think you have enough glue?"

Collette stared at the broken lamp, then up at Stevie's face. He was looking at her with so much hope, like he thought she could fix anything.

"Sure, Stevie." She walked upstairs and sat down on the top step. Stevie sat down beside her, smelling of brownies and sunshine.

"Thanks, Collette. Are you sure we have enough glue?"

Collette put her arm around her little brother and smiled.

"Positive, Stevie. We have plenty."

About the Author

Colleen O'Shaughnessy McKenna began her writing career as a child, when she sent off a script for the *Bonanza* series. McKenna is best known for her popular Murphy books, the inspiration for which comes from her own family.

This is Ms. McKenna's tenth book for Scholastic Hardcover and her eighth Murphy book. Her previous titles include: *Too Many Murphys*; *Fourth Grade Is a Jinx*; *Fifth Grade: Here Comes Trouble*; *Eenie, Meanie, Murphy, No!*; *Murphy's Island*; *The Truth About Sixth Grade*; and *Mother Murphy*.

In addition to the Murphy series, Ms. McKenna has written *Merry Christmas, Miss McConnell!* and the young adult novel *The Brightest Light*.

A former elementary school teacher, Ms. McKenna lives in Pittsburgh, Pennsylvania, with her husband and four children.

APPLE® PAPERBACKS

Pick an Apple and Polish Off Some Great Reading!

BEST-SELLING APPLE TITLES

❑ MT43944-8	**Afternoon of the Elves**	Janet Taylor Lisle	$2.75
❑ MT43109-9	**Boys Are Yucko**	Anna Grossnickle Hines	$2.95
❑ MT43473-X	**The Broccoli Tapes**	Jan Slepian	$2.95
❑ MT42709-1	**Christina's Ghost**	Betty Ren Wright	$2.75
❑ MT43461-6	**The Dollhouse Murders**	Betty Ren Wright	$2.75
❑ MT43444-6	**Ghosts Beneath Our Feet**	Betty Ren Wright	$2.75
❑ MT44351-8	**Help! I'm a Prisoner in the Library**	Eth Clifford	$2.95
❑ MT44567-7	**Leah's Song**	Eth Clifford	$2.75
❑ MT43618-X	**Me and Katie (The Pest)**	Ann M. Martin	$2.95
❑ MT41529-8	**My Sister, The Creep**	Candice F. Ransom	$2.75
❑ MT40409-1	**Sixth Grade Secrets**	Louis Sachar	$2.95
❑ MT42882-9	**Sixth Grade Sleepover**	Eve Bunting	$2.95
❑ MT41732-0	**Too Many Murphys**	Colleen O'Shaughnessy McKenna	$2.75

Available wherever you buy books, or use this order form.

Scholastic Inc., P.O. Box 7502, 2931 East McCarty Street, Jefferson City, MO 65102

Please send me the books I have checked above. I am enclosing $_____ (please add $2.00 to cover shipping and handling). Send check or money order — no cash or C.O.D.s please.

Name _____

Address _____

City_____ State/Zip _____

Please allow four to six weeks for delivery. Offer good in the U.S.A. only. Sorry, mail orders are not available to residents of Canada. Prices subject to change.

APP59

APPLE Classics

Available wherever you buy books, or use this order form.